Eighteenpence

R. E. Obeng

Original manuscript edited with notes by

KARI DAKO
Department of English, University of Ghana, Legon

SUB-SAHARAN PUBLISHERS
LEGON, ACCRA
1998

This Edition First Published by
Sub-Saharan Publishers
P. O. Box 358
Legon, Ghana

© R. E. Obeng

ISBN 9988–550–14–6

Designed and Typeset by Woeli Publishing Services, Accra

Table of Contents

Foreword to the First Edition

THIS IS an immeasurably important book and I consider it a great privilege to have been invited by its gifted author to read the galley proofs and to write the foreword.

This book is important because it marks a new epoch in Gold Coast approach to English literature. It is the first long novel in English ever published by a Gold Coast man. Casely Hayford's *Ethiopia Unbound* which, in a way, was an imaginative story was political in motive. *Eighteenpence* is a true novel in the sense of a fictitious prose tale concerned with the more sensitive passions of the human heart: love and ambition; tragedy and comedy; the success or the failure of a life.

Secondly, the book is important because, whatever may be said of its author, he is a born story-teller. He brings joy to the heart of many because he has the gift for entertainment. Such men are rare in Gold Coast public life and R. E. Obeng must be a welcome find.

And, in the third place *Eighteenpence* is important as a possible forerunner of many great works — let us hope — by Mr. Obeng and by other Gold Coast men and women who should be proud to follow the trail he has blazed.

Henry Fielding, with his Tom Jones, opened the way for the coming of the distinctive English novel in which men and women were seen without exaggeration plying their daily trades under the eye of an impartial observer who could penetrate their secret motives. In a large measure R. E. Obeng does the same for the Gold Coast with his *Eighteenpence.*

The book has a plot, but that is not its chief merit. The outstanding quality of *Eighteenpence* is its emotional treatment of certain commonplace situations in Gold Coast life, with in-dications of what future improvements in these situations might be. The farmer, the trader, the police constable, the school teacher, the lawyer, the chief, the judicial and political officer, even our young daughters: Violet, Lily and Rose, nay, even the husbands and the wives — both those who are 'better halves' and those who are only 'better quarters' or some other aliquot part of their husbands — and those who have to share their husbands with other women — each one of these typical men and women in the Gold Coast will find a picture of himself or herself in this book, for better or for worse.

And yet the book is not didactic. Like the pleasant flow of a brook on the high peaks of the Kwahu mountain, where most of the scenes are laid, the book teaches without seeming to teach; it flows, without seeming to flow. It tells the story of a man who, reduced to the last dregs of life, at last found inspiration in what a matchet could do for him.

Akrofi, the hero, was prepared to work his fingers to the bone, even to enslave himself in order to make a living; but in addition, he sought knowledge and instruction, and he thought also of new ways and ideas to make farming both a pleasure and a paying proposition. Mother earth was responsive, even generous and at last success came — material and spiritual — wealth, happiness, contentment, opportunity for doing good to others and eventually a happy home adorned with a good wife and three really lovely daughters: Violet, Lily and Rose.

Unfortunately, Akrofi had an uncle too, a never-do-well wanderer, who, after vainly exploring all his little world, came home to his now wealthy nephew Akrofi, not, however, to roost, but to disperse and to bring tragedy.

But the appearance of the bad uncle in Akrofi's life is only an episode and intermezzo, connecting one phase of Akrofi's prosperity to another.

The end of the story is almost like a fairy tale. After the bad uncle had disappeared, as all bad uncles eventually do, the hero came back into his own with an abundance of wealth undreamt of in the dreams of any Gold Coast Croesus.

As to style of the book, it must seem an amazing thing that such an effort is possible in the Gold Coast. But it *seems* so only. Mr. Obeng's command of choice English should be no cause of surprise to those who know what Gold Coast men can do when once they set their heart on any venture. With superb ease- R. E. Obeng tells his story in a mode of the King's English that would live for long years — not merely for the sake of the story but for the beauty of his style and the sonorous cadence of his music. Mr Obeng's English has vigour, balance and poise. Humour and pathos abound in the book.

There are limitations, of course. Whilst completely at home when describing procedure in an Akan court, Mr. Obeng, not being a habitue of the English courts, does as well as in the circumstances might be expected of a layman. But one of the many joys of the book is certainly the opening speeches of counsel at the trial of Akrofi on a charge of 'stealing' a treasure-trove found on his land. The hero, of course, was acquitted, thereupon his life became one sweet crescendo of success, until the bad uncle came.

Eighteenpence should earn easily its place as the first Gold Coast Classic of its kind.

J. B. DANQUAH.
Castle Road, Adabraka, Accra

October 1941

vii

Acknowledgements

THE FOLLOWING are acknowledged for their help and encouragment in making this new edition of *Eighteenpence* possible.

Madam Rose Obeng, who as the daughter of Rosina Nyanta and R. E. Obeng, is the eldest surviving offspring of the author. 'Auntie Rose' spoke to me for many an hour and gave invaluable information about her late father's life.

Mr. F. E. Obeng, 'Lawyer Obeng', is Auntie Rose's younger brother. He was able to give very detailed information on the family.

Mr. E. E. Obeng to whom I am extremely grateful, especially since he allowed me to interview him during a period of ill health. Mr. E. E. Obeng, formerly of the Ghana Publishing Corporation, was instrumental in getting *Eighteenpence* published in Ghana in 1971/72.

Mr. K. E. Obeng, R. E. Obeng's youngest son, who is a Judge in Botswana, showed great interest in the project and supplied some of the written background material.

Mr. Charles Yaw Koranteng, who is the son of R. E. Obeng's nephew Opanin Onwona-Agyemang. Opanin Onwona lived in Kuru Memorial Villa which his uncle, R. E. Obeng, had built with his mother's money and in her memory. It was because Mr. Koranteng looked after his father in his old age, and as a result lived in Kuru Memorial Villa, that some of R. E. Obeng's original papers were salvaged. I must in the same vein thank my husband, Prof. D. Y. Dako, an 'Aduanaba', who facilitated the collection of all the material and liaised with R. E. Obeng's only living trustee, Mr. F. E. Obeng, to grant publishing rights for this new edition.

I also wish to thank the Aduana clan of Abetifi for their goodwill towards me and their help and interest in the project.

Introduction

Kari Dako

EIGHTEENPENCE is the first true novel to be published by a Gold Coaster[1]. R. E. Obeng, a native of Abetifi, Kwahu, wrote the novel as a pensioner living out his retirement years in his hometown. It is a novel written with two aims: to instruct and to entertain. As a retired person, Obeng became a prolific writer. Several Twi manuscripts were discovered recently, but of these only *Tete Romafo Akokodrufo* was ever published. Additionally a collection of aphorisms: *Over One Thousand Maxims* came out in 1943. Sadly two manuscripts written in English appear lost. Mr E. E. Obeng remembers typing out one manuscript in the early forties: a collection of detective stories called *Issa Busanga*. Correspondence with Obeng's publishers in Britain contain references to a text called *Triple Tragedy*. Neither of these manuscripts can be traced.

Eighteenpence was first published by the British publisher Arthur H. Stockwell, Ltd. in 1943; then again by Willmer Bros. & Co. Ltd in 1950; and by the Ghana Publishing Corporation in 1971. The novel has since been out of print. Obeng financed his own publications in Britain and arranged his own distribution and advertisement. In a *Memorandum of Agreement* between Arthur H. Stockwell, Ltd., and the author, dated 8 July 1938, we read:

> THE PUBLISHERS undertake to print the MSS by the AUTHOR at present entitled "EIGHTEENPENCE" in suit-

---

[1] Casely Hayford's *Ethiopia Unbound* published in 1911 is by some scholars considered the first novel in the The Gold Coast and in West Africa for that matter, but although the book does contain novelistic aspects, I would not necessarily classify it as as a true novel.

*able type nicely arranged and to machine on good antique paper a first edition of 1000 copies **after necessary considerable literary revision by their Editor** (emphasis mine).*
THE BOOK to be bound as sales demand in an attractive cloth cover with gold on coloured lettering to the approval of the AUTHOR and to be wrapped in a paper (panel) jacket and to be priced at 5/-d (five shillings) net per copy.

THE AUTHOR has paid the sum of £13 (thirteen pounds) cash . . . and further agrees to pay the balance of £65 (sixty-five pounds) . . . thus completing in all a total payment by the AUTHOR to the PUBLISHERS of £78 (seventy-eight pounds) . . .

The author thus paid £78 to have his novel published in an edition of 1000 copies. The war delayed publication somewhat, and it was not until 1943 that the book actually appeared. Then in 1949, Obeng was in contact with Willmer Bros. & Co Ltd., another publisher-printer. This time he wanted an initial 2000 copies of *Eighteenpence*. The publisher quotes a price of £256.10.0. The selling price according to the jacket was now 6/- (six shillings). The books were shipped to the Gold Coast[2] and arrived in Abetifi a couple of months after R. E. Obeng's death, on 17th February 1951.

That we can now publish the manuscript once again is of great importance, because this time, an older text is available. For the sake of convenience, we will call this older, original text: text 'A' and the revised, newer text used by the former publishers: text' B'. The author, feeling conscious about his use of English, actually asked the publishers in Britain to revise the language of *Eighteenpence*. When we compare the two texts: the more recent is definitely more polished, it does not have the unexpected

---

[2] The invoice is dated 24 March 1951

vocabulary item[3] that somehow gives the impression of having been taken straight out of a thesaurus; it does not contain the elaborate sentence structures that give the impression of hyper-correctness; it no longer has any inappropriate similes, nor has Obeng's more profuse euphemistic outpourings been retained. Yet the editor of this new edition feels that the recently discovered manuscript ('A') should be published. This was the manuscript that R. E. Obeng himself wanted in print. When the two manuscripts differ noticeably, manuscript 'B' is referred to in the footnotes. It has been attempted throughout the book to strike a balance between Obeng's language and acceptable standard usage. The decision what to leave untouched and what to edit has at times been difficult. The reader must judge whether the right choices have been made.

In addition to J. B. Danquah's *Foreword to the first Edition*, this new edition also contains some recently discovered autobiographical notes. These needed extensive editing and are added to throw more light on the author himself and additionally to give the reader a better insight into the historical circumstances that made Obeng what he became. We now know that he probably was born in 1877 and not in 1868 as was previously thought. We get some interesting historical information about the early missionaries in Abetifi, about the building of the Basel Mission Station and about the early converts. R. E. Obeng's autobiographical notes are also interesting from the point of what they contain and what they omit. We are given a fairly basic account of his childhood and his early years as a teacher in the Basel Mission Church Education Service. We are given detailed accounts of his postings: 7 postings in 10 years. His marriage breaks up, he resigns and prepares to join the Government Teaching Service. The sacrifice and subsequent alienation of this early

---

[3] For example, in 'A' Chapter VIII, par. 3, Konaduwa is referred to as 'the swarthy woman'. Obviously this was a wrong choice of vocabulary and so 'B', Chapter VII, par. 5 has 'the attractive woman.'

Christian acolyte can only be guessed at. Straddling two cultures, he did not feel at ease in any. This theme of the early teacher/catechist constantly being moved and reposted, unable to settle, and consequently the breakdown of marriage and family is central to early Ghanaian novels, for example *The Narrow Path* by Francis Selormey.

From interviews with his surviving children, we know that Obeng resigned from the Basel Mission Service because he had fathered a child outside marriage.

> *'Because of some domestic affairs . . . I was asked by the Local Committe to go home to settle a dispute between me and my wife. It resulted in the dissolution of the marriage . . .*
>
> *The following July, I was married to another woman with whom I worked at Domeabra for two years.'*

The Church demanded of its converts and especially its employees that they maintain a Christian and conjugal marriage. This was alien to Akan custom, but more so, the church itself added to the stress of this domestic arrangement, by low remuneration, constant transfers and the demand that 'European' standards be kept in dress, discipline and attitude. And so R. E. Obeng was compelled to leave, and a teacher-cum-catechist who had served his employer, the Basel Mission, diligently for over 10 years, and had attestations and results to show for it[4] receives rather cool testimonials with offensive recommendations from the church representatives. Rev. Otto Shimming states that *'as far as I know, he can also be trusted'*, and Rev. C. E. Martinson recommends him as *'obedient and submissive . . . '* Clearly Obeng included these to demonstrate that colonialism was in its essence dehumanising and oppressive.

---

[4] Refer to several quoted inspection reports in the Autobiography.

And so Obeng continued his life as a Euro-christian educator, but in the Government Teaching Service. He founded Juaso Boys' School. The moralistic prying of the church was now less confining, and so Obeng lived out his life blending the two cultures: Akan and European, in his own domestic arrangements. In all he had fourteen children with various women: most of whom he married traditionally — yet he keeps referring in his correspondence to his 'matrimonial' wife. This was Rosina Janet Nyanta, his child-hood girlfriend from Abetifi who was additionally his 'second legal wife'. She was the silent witness to Obeng's obvious weakness for younger women. She brought up his many children and suffered the slights from his nephews. The final insult to this obviously very warm and soft-spoken woman, was Obeng's marriage to the very young Christiana Donkor upon his return to Abetifi as a pensioner. Rosina's relatives wanted to take Obeng to court for bigamy over this, but Rosina, a very private person, had suffered enough public attention, having had to return to her mother's house in Abetifi, while Obeng built a modern bungalow for himself and his new wife. But then Obeng's relationship with women had never been easy. This is clearly seen in the female characters he created in *Eighteenpence*. Konaduwa is a very beautiful yet strong steamroller of a woman who describes herself adrogynously as a 'masculine woman' and who overcomes all and everything in her path[5]. As a complete foil he creates Akrofi's wife. She is not named and is allowed to utter only two inconsequentialities in the whole of Part II of the novel where she features. Her daughters by Akrofi are three foreign flowers: Rose, Lily and Violet, totally alien in the context of Akan society.

R. E. Obeng had a very strong mother and grandmother. His only sibling was his sister Susana Abena Kesewaa. She left much of the responsibility for the upbringing of her children to

---

[5] Refer Konaduwa's utterances before the District Commissioner and the Adontenhene as quoted below.

Obeng. He was unusually strict in the treatment of his daughters. Interestingly, while Obeng's own children, with no exception, benefited from the schooling and education their father could give them, Obeng's two nephews who were to inherit him, became in many ways wasters and are described as such in his will.

Obeng's mother was Nana Akua Kuru Animwaa. The impression given by her son in his autobiographical notes is that she was a farmer and some-time domestic help at the mission. In actual fact she was a wealthy trader in charge of a large band of carriers. She bought slaves at Salaga. These were, upon the abolition of domestic slavery, adopted into the Aduana clan and stayed with her till she died in 1925. By then Akua Kuru had taken on the name Maria to signify her conversion to Christianity, and she was an Elder of the Church. Already in 1890, she had bought a large parcel of land in what is today Christian Quarters in Abetifi, and she left other substantial wealth. It was with the inheritance from his mother, that Obeng built Kuru Memorial Villa at Abetifi in her memory.

Eighteenpence was originally planned as a moral fable. The protagonist Akrofi was through hard work and the willingness to adopt 'modernity': to metamorphose from an improverished youngster to an exceedingly rich man. He was to be tested and to undergo trials in order to emerge victorious in the end. But this is not how the book ended up. In many ways Obeng sabotaged his own creation. The supposed villain: Konaduwa, in a way hi-jacks the story and becomes the main character. Akrofi ends up as a satirised semblance of what the author initially intended him to be. Structurally, the novel has two distinct parts; for convenience they will be called Part I and Part II. Whereas Konaduwa reigns supreme in Part I, Akrofi is the hero (yet in many ways the antihero[6]) of Part II. Contemporary society is

---

[6] Obeng set out to write a moral fable with Akrofi as the hero, yet the author in many ways sabotages his own creation so that Akrofi receives less of our sympathy as we get to know more about him.

in transition; two judicial systems: the Colonial and the Traditional operate side by side and are not necessarily complementary to each other. The Colonial Administration is alien and not trusted. Crafty lawyers[7] and clever twisting of arguments[8] win court cases. The traditional court is viewed as extortionate[9]. Part I is set in Abetifi and the contemporary social scenery is described in great ethnographic detail. The main character is the woman Konaduwa, the traditional Akan woman whose cantankerous yet courageous voice is heard in all fora in the Colony: traditional and modern. She is made the voice of the Kwahus. As a woman she can speak what no man dares, she thus can address the District Commissioner in the following manner:

> *"Is this what the English Court is like? " she demanded with astonishment. "When a case has not been tried, how can one say whether one is guilty or not? Even if the case has been tried, how can you expect one to pronounce judgement against oneself?"*
> *. . . "If you asked me this question a hundred times, I will*

---

[7] Refer the Omanhene' s case against Akrofi at the High Court, Accra. Certainly **right** did not win the case, but the craftiness of the lawyer.

[8] Refer Konaduwa's utterances before the D. C. and the Adontenhene. Neither court obviously could handle this woman who upset the *status quo*, she is therefore described as 'mad' and her case eventually dismissed with her being labelled as 'jealous'.

[9] The novel is set in Abetifi in the reign of an historical Adotenhene and the narration starts in 1913. At this time Kwahu had emerged from Ashanti overlordship, but had been incorporated into the Gold Coast Colony in 1901. The state coffers were empty. While the chiefs and elders wanted to maintain their traditional Akan predominance within the parameters possible under the colonial hegemony: judiciary and economic power, the commoners wanted to break the extortionary judicial practices of the chiefs and gain representation on the traditional councils. Consequently, the period 1905–1930 experienced 3 destoolments and 3 abdications in the paramountcy of Kwahu.

still make no reply. Even if I knew I were guilty, I should never admit it and ask you to pronounce judgement upon me. If I say I am not guilty, you would not let me go scot free; but if I say I am guilty, you would pronounce judgement at once."

"Do not waste my time," the Commissioner ordered.
"If you have not time, why do you say you will settle cases? You are not cultivating or trading for the Government, but you receive a good salary each month. Perhaps your pay is much higher than your father's in your country. You have nothing to do but sit in your office, come to court and ask one or two questions, and go back to eat and sleep, yet you get your pay. If I want to ask a thousand questions, I will, and you cannot hush me."

Before the Adontenhene's court in the presence of the Omanhene she proclaims:

"Every knife is out when the bull is down! If I were not a woman I would tell you that you seem to have time to spare — no, to waste. If the District Commissioner could not settle a case, then which of you here has the power to settle it? Let me ask you this, or remind you, or awaken you, if you are sleeping. In the old days when our ancestors judged their cases in Kumasi, was any case sent back from there so that you might judge it and inflict punishment?". . .
"I will make no defence and if you can judge the case and punish me when I have not spoken, be sure that there is a court much higher than this, to which I will appeal."

These rather lengthy quotes have been included to show that Obeng uses Konaduwa to attack both the colonial administration and the Akan oligarchy.

Part II is a very different narrative. The author attempts

a more novelistic form and takes more definite control over the unfolding of the story. The result is a rather flat linear narrative. The protagonist is male, his wife a nameless appendix and their lifestyle is definitely 'modern'. Akrofi, the illiterate nonentity who speaks pidgin to the Europeans and refers to them as his 'master' has created a realm of his own that is a mirror of the colonial plantation: Akrofi is the lord of the manor and foreigners i.e. non-Akans do the work. This modern utopia is an upside down world, in which the Omanhene loses a case in an alien court to a person who has the slur of indebtedness and slavery attached to him.

The book is as readable and relevant today as it was when it was first published. The 1950 edition had the following write-up on its jacket, a good summary of what the book is all about:

> *A most original novel of the Gold Coast. Humour and pathos abound, and a vivid picture is presented of Gold Coast life — the people, courtship and marriage, family life, customs, laws, and the conditions of climate and country.*
>
> *Dr. J. B. Danquah, in the foreword, acclaims "Eighteenpence" to be unique because it is the first long novel in English ever published by a Gold Coast man, and because of its outstanding quality in its emotional treatment of certain commonplace situation in Gold Coast life. The novel, Dr. Danquah says, "should earn easily its place as the first Gold Coast classic of its kind."*

The Autobiography of the Author

I, RICHARD EMMANUEL OBENG, was born in Abetifi, in Kwahu, in the 1870's. It is supposed to have been on the 14 October 1877 because of certain events which happened at that time. My father was Daniel Kwadwo (Donko) Asare, a native of Akropong, Akuapem, and my mother was Maria Akua (Kuru) Animwa of Abetifi, Kwahu.

In 1869, the Rev Frederick Augustus Ramsayer and Mrs. Ramsayer were led from Anum, in the Volta District, to Kumasi as captives of war[1]. Their captors halted at Abetifi for about six weeks[2]. There the obliging inhabitants treated the white captives with exceptional kindness. They presented them with bananas, pine-apples, eggs and other foodstuffs. As the Ramsayers were the first white men seen by them, the people of Abetifi looked on them with all wonder and awe, taking them to be spirits or gods. Mr. and Mrs. Ramsayer were pleased with the exceptional kindness shown them by the people, and Mr. Ramsayer, then a lay man, made a vow that if God spared his life and released him from his bondage, he would return to Abetifi with the Gospel as a means of showing gratitude to the kind people of Abetifi.

In February 1874, after four years' captivity in Kumasi, the Ramsayers were released by Sir Joseph Wolsely, when he defeated the Ashantis on the 4th February and burnt their capital on the 6 February in the eventful reign of Otumfuo Kofi Karikari.

---

[1] This was during the "Krepi" war.

[2] According to Ramsayer: Ramsayer, F. A. & J. Kühne 1878 *Four Years in Ashantee*, London: James Nisbert & Co; they must have rested only for a day.

This Asantehene, on account of his exceptional kindness to his subjects, was given the appellation *AKYEMPO*, meaning *he who presented nuggets.*

To fulfil his solemn promise, two years after their liberation from captivity, in 1876, after he had been ordained, the Rev. Ramsayer and his wife were again seen in Abetifi, accompanied by the Rev. Weimer, the Rev. Werner and the Catechist Kofi Suaah, a native of Kyebi, Akyem-Abuakwa. They were no more prisoners of war, but preachers of the Gospel.

The missionaries were not warmly welcomed. They were unfavourably received by both the Omanhene, Akuamoah Kwaku Adofo and the Adontenhene, Kofi Dankyi Awere I, because these had heard that Christianity gives back the freedom of both slaves and subjects. The missionaries, however, were not discouraged, and their zeal for the intended work not an inch abated. They were housed at Kubease, under the roof of Elder Yaw Preko, nicknamed *Preko Babaawa* because of his personal beauty, who took care of them. They held their services and meetings in the town under the canopy of the blue sky and amidst a sea of strange faces.

After a considerable time, as their services were greatly disturbed by the extra and unwelcome noises, and seeing that their landlord and the people were casting evil looks on them, the missionaries made up their mind to have a plot of land to build their own station outside the town. A hilly piece of land at Kurokosiwa, near the Odwenase Street was earmarked by them, but the local Elders did not agree, because it was known that wherever missionaries reside, they rear goats and cattle, and as the goat is a bitter enemy of their fetish Tanno, it was feared that the goats would come into the town, and thereby defile their fetishes, which pollution would arouse the intense anger of their gods. The missionaries were therefore shifted from the lovely spot they had chosen, and a higher hill was given to them at Oboyang for the sum of *Bennaa,* in those days equivalent to £7.6s 0d. It is situated at the northern edge of town. The road to this new plot went through the public cemetery, which was thickly overgrown, and therefore both difficult and scary to pass through, especially after dark.

The missionaries did not like the spot, though the site was very good and much better than the first. They therefore raised several objections, but as it is ill to stay in Rome and strive with the Pope, they were prevailed upon by the Elders, and so the land was cleared.

The missionaries were the first to bring silver coins to Kwahu. Many labourers were engaged, who worked from morning till evening, and who were paid at the rate of nine pence per day. Some were paid in salt and others in tobacco or blue. Before the modern money economy, iron rods and especially cowries were the money exchanged at the market. The silver coin of three pence was exchanged for five farthing ($1^1/_4$d), because the labourers considered cowries more valuable than three pence. In those days, thirty-five cowries was equal to one farthing.

The number of labourers increased daily, and before long, a greater part of the land was cleared and a swish building with three rooms built for the missionaries to live in. This was the first such building in the whole country. At the same time, another building containing two rooms was built for Mr. Kofi Suaah, the Catechist.

In the course of time, work on the storey building which was to serve as permanent dwelling place for the missionaries was started. The house was planned as three-storied, but the third fell as often as they erected it, so they abandoned the idea and ended up with a two-storied building[3].

Locally, there were no carpenters nor sawyers nor bricklayers who could work about this huge building, so artisans were hired from Akuapem, and among them came my dear father, who was a sawyer by profession. Then and there my father saw my mother, who was a young and beautiful woman. They fell

---

[3] This building is still standing in Abetifi.

in love with one another, were married, and I am the outcome of their marriage.

When I was about nine months old, I was attacked by dropsy[4] in both shoulders. Several native medicines were fruitlessly applied, but I fell unconscious. As the sickle of death cuts down the green as oft as the ripe, my span of life was almost abridged in babyhood. My dearly beloved mother shrieked and wailed and made a doleful noise, thinking the sickness would prove fatal. She ran, totally distraught, to the house of a fetish priest and herbalist called Anno Kofi and asked for his assistance, even if it would cost her her life, a pledge she strengthened with oath.

The kind man promised to do all in his power to restore the circulation of blood, provided that God helped him in his arduous enterprise. My mother's anguish was so great, that she nearly died. She could hardly breathe and sank rather than sat down on the floor, because she was close to collapse and was about to faint. But she rallied and became herself again: acting totally unrestrained: rolling herself on the floor and shouting she would die with me if the herbalist could not restore my life. Meanwhile some herbs had been collected by the herbalist. These he put together with a good deal of pepper and onions in a vessel containing live coals. I was then held head and face downwards over this vessel. Smoke engulfed me, I sneezed, and my circulation was restored, and I became alive again like one resurrected from the dead. You can imagine how glad my mother was when she saw me breathing again. I was put on her lap to suck her milky breast again. The joyful news spread quickly far and wide, and people rushed in to see me and to congratulate my mother on my remarkable recovery.

My coffin, which was by then ready, was given to the herbalist before whom all now stood in awe and admiration. In order

---

4   R. E. Obeng had a shorter right arm: slightly crippled. It is possible that what he describes here is an attack of poliomyelitis.

to confuse the evil spirits, a clothed piece of banana stem was put in the coffin while the herbalist continued to treat me till I was entirely healed. That coffin which is now converted into a box is still in the old man's room and it is still known as *Obeng fundaka* meaning "Obeng's coffin". When I was fully well again, the price agreed in the bargain was paid by my mother.

When I was still young and unconscious of myself, according to the information of my mother, I used to pick up bits of paper and leaves and look at them, pretending to be reading and hushed or waved my hand to any person who would laugh or make noise. This made them think that I was born a school-boy, and so they prepared to send me to school when my age would permit.

My father left Kwahu and went to his own home at Akropong when I was still young. When I grew a little I saw that my mother used to take me pick-aback to the Mission Station, where she was engaged in cleaning the window panes of the mission house for wages. Biscuits, lumps of sugar and slices of bread were given to me always by Mrs Ramsayer. Once I was even honoured with a gown made of coloured cuttings of cloth, which dress I dearly priced above anything, and I wished there were no nights to cause me to take it off. In the morning I rose very early before cock-crow and often aroused my mother to get me dressed in my new finery.

When the missionaries visited the town, children scampered after them and shouted '*Yɛ Owura, yɛ owura* ' i.e. "Our master, our master"; some added '*Ma yɛ paano,*' meaning "Give us some biscuits", but when the Europeans turned towards the children, off they went tumbling in fright.

The wise missionaries then made a scheme to make a "Free School" in the town beside the Boarding School at the Station, because the children in the town were much afraid to go there on account of the "white men".

Nana Kofi Dankyi, the Adontenhene, who knew the good work done by the missionaries on the Coast, when he went to

Accra on behalf of the whole State in the year 1874 to embrace the British Flag, now loved them dearly and treated them with every kindness. Unfortunately six years later, in 1883, the Adontenhene died and was succeeded by his nephew Nana Kwame Addo, who was invited from Krakye where he had lived as a hostage with Dente for many years. The new Adontenhene too was on friendly terms with the missionaries though some times he was passionate and overbearing. The missionaries told him about their concern about children to feed the school in town. He asked them to send one of their teachers into town to teach the children there. Consequently, every morning at nine o'clock, a hand-bell was rung in the streets of the town. Whenever we heard the sound of the bell, we flocked behind the ringer all round the town until he was asked by the schoolmaster to stop.

The school boys at the Mission Station were periodically supplied with cotton uniforms and often times they were seen dressed in them with turkey-red cummerbunds round their waists. These cummerbunds were the magnet which attracted many children into the school. It was that which also attracted me.

One day when my mother and my grand-mother had gone to their farm, I followed the boy who was ringing the bell to the school in town. I was then about six or seven years old. The school was being kept at Kubease, in the house of Elder Kwabene Oboe, the successor of Preko Babaawa, the very house in which the missionaries were housed when they first arrived. When I was in another room opposite to the schoolroom, the teacher noticed that I was paying particular attention to what he was teaching. He asked my name and called me. I was more than glad when he called me for I knew he was going to ask me if I liked to be enrolled. And so he did. He asked if I wished to go to school. I answered in the affirmative and at once without consulting my parents or guardian, I was enrolled to my greatest pleasure. The teacher then gave me a slate and a pencil, gratis, for that was the custom in those days.

When my mother and my grand-mother returned in the

afternoon, they saw the slate hanging on the wall. My grand-
mother hastily asked whose it was; and I replied boldly that it
was mine. They were both greatly disturbed, and the old lady
at once shed tears for the following reasons:

(i) The fetish of the priest who cured me would say
my mother was ungrateful to have sent me to school,
and they feared the fetish might cause another sick
ness which might be fatal, and no assistance could
be got.

(ii) We have a fetish in our family which is called Tanno.
This, they feared, might kill me if the other fetish
spared my life, for they had heard that missionaries
and their teachers forced their pupils to speak against the fetish and to embrace their new religion,
even if the pupils did not like to.

(iii) They had heard that the teachers flogged the children
if they could not do their lessons, and as I was too
feeble and delicate, they feared they might flog me
to death.

(iv) The people who were educated seldom stayed in
their native towns, and nor would I if they allowed
me to go to school.

These and other reasons instigated them to persuade me to send
the "white man's stone" back to the schoolmaster by another boy,
as they were afraid he would do me some harm if I went in person.
But I was not to be persuaded, so they adopted a new method,
which consisted of threats and starvation. Often times no food
was prepared for me when I came home; but being determined,
I continued to attend school with punctuality and regularity.
When they saw that my wish to go to school was impregnable,
they yielded.

After one year's course in this "Town School", as it was
called, we were examined by the Rev. Fr. Ramsayer, and luckily,

I was among the successful boys who were promoted to the next higher class at the Station. I continued to Infant Class II and Class III in 1887, when my father returned to Kwahu and took me away with him to Akuapem. On our way to Akuapem, we heard of the death of Nana Amoako Atta I, the Omanhene of Akyem-Abuakwa, at Kyebi. He was known for his persecution of the Christians in his country. On account of his death, my father, who had become a Court-Crier of Nana Kwame Fori, the Omanhene of Akuapem, daubed me and himself with red clay and put his official cap made of gold and monkey skin on a silver chain round my neck so that it rested on my chest. He explained that the people of Akyem would kill us if we went without these visible signs. After about one week's journey, we arrived at Bewease, where his farm was, and where I was fated to live for one full year without attending school.

In the year 1888, my maternal uncle, Kwadwo Yeboah, arrived to take me back to Kwahu. I was delighted. A few days after our arrival, I visited the school. The Rev. Samuel Kwafo, then a Catechist, was in charge of the school. My class-mates who saw me from the window told the schoolmaster all about me. On the following Sunday he came to the town to see my mother and grand-mother whom he asked to send me back to school. They asked him to enquire from me whether I was willing to go to school again; and when I readily answered "Yes", they rebuked me when the school master had gone. Early on Monday morning, the school master, accompanied by a few boys, came to take me to school. My mother told him I had no "white man's stone" nor pencil nor book, so he should go back and come back another time. The school master, however, answered that he had all these things ready for me at the school. My mother's intention was to have time to consult our family fetish whether it would be safe if I went back to school. Seeing that all her entreaties were fruitless, she angrily said: "There he sits, if you take him to school and he sickens or dies, do not let me hear of it". The schoolmaster agreed not to inform her should I die in school that day, and so we marched off to the Station.

My class mates had been promoted to Standard I, and I was put in Infants III again. Our subjects of instruction were: *reading, writing, arithmetic, and religious instruction.* At the first mission anniversary held in Abetifi on the 28 October 1890, I was baptized by the Rev. Fr. Ramsayer with the name Richard, to which I added Emmanuel afterwards. Successfully and regularly I passed Standards I and II until in July 1891 with three other boys: Theodore Ewart Asante, Benjamin Franklin Ansong and David Okata, I passed Standard III and we were promoted to Standard IV in Begoro Basel Mission Middle School, as the school was then called, under the management of the Rev. Andreas Philip Bauer, now of sacred memory. The teachers were: the Headmaster, now the Rev. David R. Ansong, master, now the Rev. Martin A. Adade and Master Henry, now of sacred memory.

On the the 20 October 1891, my dear grand-mother died at Abetifi. The news of her death reached me a few days afterwards, and I was granted one day's leave to mourn her.

In July, 1892, the headmaster Mr. D. R. Ansong was transferred and Mr Joshua Ayeh, now ordained minister, took his charge. Mr. Henry Ansong was also tranferred and Mr. Charles Emmanuel Ewi replaced him. Under these able masters we passed Standards IV and V with ease, and in January 1893, we were admitted into Standard VI where we began to study Greek for the ministry. I do not want to exaggerate or deliver self-praise, but I was always among the "Group A" of my class and so I was greatly loved by my teachers, the principal and his other staff. I must also mention that Rev. Fr. Ramsayer out of his own purse bore all the expenses of my education at this school, even though my relatives could have done so. I am very grateful to him!

I must state that up to 1892, classes were changed in July, when new teachers were consecrated at the Theological Seminary, Akropong. But because of the rains, travelling was so tedious that the local Committee of the Basel Mission Society decided to alter the system. Therefore in that year, children remained only six months in their classes.

In December 1894, we passed Standard VII, and we, thirteen in number, were all admitted into the Theological Seminary at Akropong in February 1895. The Rev. William J. Rottman was Principal and the Rev. John Lehman, his European Assistant. He died in March 1896. Mr. W. T. Evans was the House Master and Mr. Henry Reynolds Ofosu of Akropong was the other Master. Mr. Ofosu was ordained a minister before he died in 1920.

At the end the first year, a teacher was dismissed at Aburi, and I was appointed by the Principal to go to take his charge temporarily. I filled that post until February 1896 when I was relieved so that I could return to the Seminary to resume my studies. I was in Aburi when I heard of the arrest and deporation of Nana Agyeman Prempeh I in January 1896.

In February 1897 we were promoted to the Catechist Seminary where we studied nothing besides the Bible, and in March that year I delivered my first sermon, based on Acts 2: 1–18. In December 1898 I sat for and passed the Government Examination of Students and Teachers for Certificates. On the Epiphany, the 6th January 1899, I with eight others was consecrated Catechist at Akropong by the Rev. William Rottman, the Principal of the Seminary. I was subsequently stationed at Abetifi as the Principal Teacher of the Junior School. The first official report of H. M. Inspector of Schools[5] was very satisfactory. On the day of inspection, my Teacher's Certificates were endorsed as under Frank Wright, the Inspector of School:

> *"The scholars in attendance at the Abetifi Mixed School in charge of Mr. R. E. Obeng have passed a highly creditable examination"*

I married in April 1900 and on the 11 January 1901, I was favoured with a son who was christened on the 27th January 1901 by the

---

[5] i.e. Her Majesty's Inspector of Schools.

Rev. L. Obrecht with the name of Richard.

At the beginning of February that year I was transferred to take charge of the school at Bompata. There too my duties were performed with diligence, and Mr. W. C. F. Robertson, the Director of Education who examined my school in February 1902, endorsed my Certificate as follows:

> *"Mr. Obeng has been in charge of the Bompata Basel Mission Mixed School for the past year. The scholars are well taught and show that he has given care and attention to his charge".*

I was suddenly transferred to Bepong soon after this examination, where I was put in charge of the congregation and of the small school. I was there for four years. The notable events which are worth mentioning were the increase of my family by the birth of two sons: Felix born on the 30th December 1902 and baptised by the Rev. J. Sitzler on the 13th March 1903 and Winfred Lawrence born on the 5th March 1905 and baptised by the Rev Otto Schimming at Nkwatia on the Pentecost Day on the 16th April 1905. The other events were the building of the Station on the Asakraka road and the laying of the foundation of the chapel on the 5th February 1903 by Rev. Edmund Perregaux.

In January 1906 I was transferred to Abetifi to take the post of House-Master of the Theological Seminary. In the following year I sat the Examination of Studies and Teachers as under Schedule "G", which I successfully passed. But I did not stay here long. In December that year I was asked to go to Anum to be in charge of the congregation and the Junior School. As the events which led to this sudden transfer were based upon the accusation of some conspirators, I declined, but after advice from my superiors, I yielded and went to Anum. Giving my valedictory sermon on Christmas day 1906, I left Abetifi with my family on the 27 December and spent the night at Tafo. On the next and following days we passed through Nkyene-nkyene;

Asubone; Dotopong; Mmankrom; Akyerem-akuraa; Asante-akuraa; Yaw Amoako; Aboho; Onyina-nkonyo; Seeso; Apebo-abomma; Onyinatia; Opirim-asuwa; Agogo; Onyina-num; Sansu-aworoso; Aboe; Mpe-asem and Dodi to Anum where we arrived at 3 p.m. on Thursday the third January 1907 after we had sailed on the Afram and on the Volta in a canoe for five days. We were received with much pleasure by the Rev. G. Martin, who was in charge of the congregation and the Rev Richard Burki who was in charge of the school. Because of some domestic affairs at the end of September, I was asked by the Local Committee to go home to settle a dispute between me and my wife. It resulted in the dissolution of the marriage. In March 1908, I was sent by the Local Committee to go to Domeabra, Asante-Akyem, to take charge of the congregation and the small school which had only three children on the roll. The following July, I was married to another woman with whom I worked at Domeabra for two years. In December 1908, I sat for and obtained a Second Class Certificate and in January 1910 I obtained by examination a Certificate for the Knowledge of Agriculture. Having now obtained all the necessary Certificates which enable a teacher to secure a post in a Government School, I in July 1910 resigned my commission in the Mission Service and went to Kumasi to fight for a post in the newly opened Government School there.

Once in Kumasi, I applied to the Director of Education through Mr. A. Gardner, the Headmaster of that school, for the vacancy of an Assistant teacher, but the application was turned down. After three months' stay in Kumasi, I obtained a vacancy on the Gold Coast regiment, W. A. F. F.[6] as "C" Company Pay Clerk. The Commanding Officer asked me for testimonials, but I had none, so on the instruction of Cpt. Barker, I applied to the Rev. O. Schimming and the Rev C. E. Martinson for some. Below are copies of the testimonials.

---

[6] West African Frontier Force

> *"I hereby certify that Mr. R. E. Obeng was in the service of the Basel Mission for nearly nine years. I moreover certify that the said Obeng was not dismissed on account of misconduct or bad behaviour but resigned out of his own wish. I can state that the said R. E. Obeng is an able man, writes and speaks a good English and as far as I know, he can also be trusted."*
>
> Abetifi (Sgd.) Otto Schimming, October the 15th 1910.

The Rev. Martinson also sent me the following testimonial:

> *"TO WHOM THIS MAY CONCERN:*
> *I do hereby certify that Mr. R. E. Obeng has worked under me as Catechist in the Service of the Basel Mission for the period of two years, after which he voluntarily resigned the work. He was both obedient and submissive, and I have the pleasure to certify that he discharged his duties with honesty and all satisfaction, and I keenly regret having lost him".*
>
> Bompata (Sgd) C. E. Martinson, Minister. 20 October, 1910.

As I was not willing to work under bond for six years' continuous service, I resigned in February 1911 and applied to the Hon. The Colonial Secretary for the vacancy of Assistant Teacher which was still pending at Kumasi Government School, and which was given to me on the 20th March 1911.

Here again I did my work as satisfactorily as I could, and in December 1915, through the persuasion of Mr. Henry Evans, the new Headmaster of the school, I sat for the new Second Class Certificate as under the New Rules, in which I was successful in obtaining the Certificate. Again in December 1916, I was qualified in Hand-and-Eye Training. I also won the First Prize for the Empire Day Address written in competition by Students and Teachers in May 1916.

In January 1918 I was transferred by the Director of Education from Kumasi Government Boys' School to open and take charge of the new school in Juaso, Asante-Akim. I left Kumasi on the 6th February and opened the new school on the 11th of that month with only seven children, without ceremony. It was opened in April with ceremony by Sir Francis Fuller, the Chief Commissioner of Ashanti, when I had enrolled 72 children. The school was extended to Standard VII in 1924 with seven boys. In that year Nana Osei Agyeman Prempeh I was repatriated, and he arrived in Kumasi in November.

Towards the end of 1927, the town Juaso was moved to its present location, near the Railway Station. The Chief of Juaso, Nana Kwabena Agyei, who succeeded Nana Kofi Danso who died on the 17th July 1925, moved to the Newtown on the 13th October 1928. A new town whose foundation was laid by Sir Charles Maxwell CMG[7] on the 21st December 1929, was built at the Newtown. This was opened by Mr. H. S. Newlands, the immediate reliever of Sir Charles Maxwell on the 30th April 1930.

In January 1937, I obtained permission to retire on pension, and on the 15th March 1938, at the Legislative Council Hall, Accra, I was awarded the Gold Coast Certificate of Honour and Badge by his Excellency the Governor Sir Arnold Wienholt Hodson, KCMG[8]. I was the first Gold Coast teacher thus honoured by His Majesty the King.

In May 1939, I was appointed the Treasurer of the Kwahu State by the State Council. I held the post up to 31st December 1942, when I resigned. In January 1943, I was asked by the State Council to write the History of the Kwahu State, at which I am still working.[9]

---

[7] Companion (of the Order) of St Michael and St George.

[8] Knight Commander of the Order of St Michael and St George.

[9] Unfortunately only remnants of this manuscript has been found.

On the 23rd September 1943, my book *Eighteenpence* appeared. The Foreword of the book was written by Dr. Danquah. Many were the encouraging congratulations which I have received from well known persona and schoolmasters.

I am still in Abetifi where God preserves me.

CHAPTER 1

The Purchase

IN THE ancient and salubrious town of Abetifi, in the country of Kwahu, in the reign of Nana Addo Kese Pamboo, there lived a man whose name was Obeng-Akrofi. Obeng, though kind-hearted, was as poor as a church rat. He was also so self-conscious that he could not approach any of his friends or relatives for anything. His property on earth, besides his only cloth[1] which was threadbare, was a small dog who followed him anywhere he went. This dog he named "Poor-no-Friend".

Akrofi wanted to ascend to that rung in life in which one is expected to be happy and merry — Marriage. As this step cannot be taken in any country without spending of much money, Akrofi was likely to be embarrassed. This prospect of embarrassment goaded him to go to a well-to-do man to ask for a loan. As it is a waste of powder to shoot the man in the moon, so also it was a waste of time for Akrofi to persuade this man to give him any money. Seeing that all his attempts were fruitless, he abandoned this idea and hit on another plan.

He now decided to farm. A few miles from the town lay a vast, dense and virgin forest belonging to no master but the Adontenhene, and which therefore, according to the Native Customs, was common to all citizens, and even all strangers who had come to stay in the town by means of immigration. The only thing that Obeng-Akrofi needed was strength and health. In order to carry out his intentions, he went to a petty-trader's store with the intention to buy a cutlass on credit. The trader

---

[1] Text B has 'loin cloth', an article of clothing not found in Ghana.

gave him one at eighteenpence, and allowed him one week to make good the account. He did not like to tell a lie as all poor people are apt to do, therefore he submissively asked the creditor to extend the time to a fortnight, which the creditor kindly did.

On a whetstone firmly fixed in the ground, the fortunate man whetted the new cutlass with all eagerness. The following day, he tried it on a large thicket belonging to his deceased grand-mother. He chose this place because it was not the season for clearing the forest. He quickly cleared a very large area; and as it was sunny, the leaves dried in a very short time. He burnt the grass, and collected the remaining charred sticks, and burnt them all to ashes.

He looked forward daily to rain as the hart pants for water. He had not then decided what to plant. Luckily, he did not have to wait too long. Barely five days later a heavy rain fell through-out the night till the small hours of the following morning. At the opening of the day, he asked his only surviving aunt for a few cobs of Indian corn[2] which he had now decided to plant. The old lady most kindly gave him ten. These he quickly bruised and soaked for four days. He then planted the grains at a good distance of eight feet apart.

On the remaining part of the farm, he contrived to plant onions. In the Kwahu country, the planting of onions was a lucrative task for women. It was lucrative, for the crop was reaped in three months, and keen buyers came from Akuapem, Akyem, Swedru, Nsabaa and many other places with bundles of cocoa bags, to buy and convey it. The price per bag varied from ninety to one hundred and twenty groats for a load of sixty pounds weight. It is an axiom, therefore, that the work was more paying than the cocoa industry, for the onion crop was reaped twice yearly. This work was seldom pursued by men, except those who were the most avaricious. As it is, poverty knows no law or alternative, therefore though this kind of work was

---

[2] Maize

not manly, Akrofi set himself to it, plugging his ears to ward off all derisive words used by the passers-by.

On the remaining part of the farm, he raised some four or five hundred mounds in which he planted tiger-nuts. This was also another pursuit which fetched money, but the cultivation entailed much more elaborate work than that of the onions. The produce was bought chiefly by the Akuapems, Fantis and the educated community.

The two weeks allowed to Akrofi by the good petty-trader for making good his account elapsed without fulfilment of the obligation. The creditor was justifiably angry, and sent his boy to Akrofi to ask for the money. The sight of the messenger brought Akrofi to his senses, for the pleasure of the work done in his farm had absorbed all his mind so that he had forgotten about this obligation. He fried some of the corn and some of the ground-nuts which he had at hand to regale the boy. When the messenger finished eating, Obeng-Akrofi sent him back to his master with a message that he would see him personally that evening and without fail. Having made several mounds for the ground nuts, and closed the day's work at about five o'clock in the evening, Akrofi went home.

CHAPTER 2

The Servitude

WHEN AKROFI had had his bath and eaten the little food left him by his aunt, he asked her to accompany him to the house of his creditor, whose name was Owusu Aduemiri, to ask him for a further extension of time for the settlement of his account. His only hope was to sell the crops of the farm which was being made, and pay him from the income, but his aunt would not go. He wept. With torrents of tears streaking on his cheeks, he went to Owusu with the boldness of a lioness robbed of her cubs, and flung himself at his feet, and most humbly told him his errand, concluding by telling Owusu that he would pawn himself to him, and do all the work of a servant until after three months when he knew full well that he could obtain money to pay him.

Owusu did not like to enslave a person on account of eighteenpence; besides, he knew that British laws emphatically suppress slave dealing of all shades, with imprisonment for seven years. He therefore held Akrofi by the hand and raised him from the ground, and told him angrily that he could not accede to such a request. But Akrofi was resolute, and faithfully promised his voluntary services on all Mondays and Saturdays until when the account was closed. To this Owusu gave his assent, and cheerfully Akrofi returned to his house.

The following day was Friday, therefore Akrofi worked hard in his farm; for he knew that for the three ensuing days he could not go there to do anything. He was not a christian so he could go and work on the intervening Sunday; but that being an *Akwasidae,* he knew that it was a universal Sabbath Day on which he must not labour.

On Saturday morning, he rose with the lark[1] and went to Owusu's house with his well-sharpened cutlass under his arm. Owusu asked Akrofi to accompany one of his wives whose name was Konaduwa to work on a farm allotted[2] to her.

Wishing that this woman would report favourably on him, Akrofi worked much harder than he did on his own farm. When the woman called him to come and eat, he hesitated to go. Not only did he work hard, he whistled and sang songs and carols. Konaduwa was so much astonished that she began to mock him. She said, "I never knew before that poverty was so bitter until to-day. How is it that on account of eighteenpence a man of your age works until when his back is going to break. Your hands will be sore and painful, and your palms so full of blisters that you cannot squeeze the water from your towel when you take your bath this evening." Akrofi did not like the words; but as one cannot speak against the Pope at Rome, he rather sh t up. He came at last to have his meal and told the woman that it was not on account of poverty, such that killed the crab on the sand, that he felt compelled to work so hard, but rather gratitude which he wished to show to his creditor Owusu for the good act done to him.

The woman said: "If you are not a fool, why should you work as if you have no feelings? Why don't you reserve the strength in you to do your own work? Don't you know that next Monday you have to come here again to do the same work?

---

[1] Obeng often uses non-Ghanaian metaphors and similies. These are obviously phrases he has picked from reading English literature. The lark in this instance is not an African bird and therefore not a good choice.

[2] Text A uses the term 'allotted to her' whereas text B has been changed to: 'to work on her farm'. This change is wrong, for Konaduwa obviously worked on a piece of land that her husband had allotted to her. Refer also J. B. Danquah *The Akim Abuakwa handbook* p. 77 " . . . the wife takes her due share in raising food-stuffs in the husand's farms for the upkeep of the household."

If you were an inch wiser, you would have preserved your strength to do your own work in your farm next Tuesday. Because of your folly, I fear you will tell my husband all the good advice I am giving you and which you resent."[3]

"If you know it is good advice," muttered Akrofi, "why do you fear that I will tell your husband?"

"What were you saying, you senseless fellow?" rattled the woman. "Are you scolding me? You know that we two are here in this farm alone, and you wish to beat me. If you like, do so, and the police will handle you."

With a tremulous voice Akrofi ejaculated: "How would I dare to beat you, my master's wife? I find that you are as dangerous as a loaded gun, and your words are as poisonous as a snake. I will no longer remain here with you. Good bye." Akrofi quickly left the farm. The woman remained in the farm until very late in the evening.

On his arrival, Akrofi went to greet his master according to custom. Owusu inquired as to the whereabouts of his wife. Akrofi told him that he left her in the farm, and nothing else. Aduemiri showed him his food which he had kept for him. This he gulped in a short time. He cleaned the dishes and then put them at their proper places; and after a short conversation about the work in the farm, Akrofi took his leave and went to his house.[4]

---

[3] Text B here has the following: 'But this is folly, and I fear . . . The interpretation could thus be that Konaduwa realised that she had spoken unwisely. Obeng, on the other hand, clearly says that Konaduwa pushes the blame of the conversation onto Akrofi. She says he is so stupid that he cannot keep things, better not said, to himself.

[4] Text B subsitutes ' . . . to his house' with 'home'. The original has been kept as it echoes contemporary usage in Ghana, but the two terms will be used interchangeably later in the book.

CHAPTER 3

The Quarrel

ABOUT SEVEN o'clock that evening, Owusu went to see if his wife had now returned from the farm, and if she had, to ask her why she failed to come or to send somebody to greet him when she arrived from the farm, according to custom. As soon as he entered the house, Konaduwa began to shower abusive words on him. Quite astonished, Owusu stood for a while and then asked: "What is the matter with you? Are you going mad or what ails you?"

"Yes, I predicted that these were the very words with hich you would welcome me. You cannot get any other suitable words to use, of course. I know I am mad; and because I am mad you suffered me to stay on your farm till so late an hour; and instead of asking me why I was unable to come home at the usual time, you call me a mad woman. Let me assure you, I am not one of your slaves whom you buy at eighteenpence each. If you had all the gold in Australia or California, you cannot buy me.[1] I swear by your father and mother and *Asase Aban* with *Fofie* and *Obonyame* on top that you must divorce me to-night. If you refuse the fetish must kill me."[2]

When Owusu heard these words, he became a Zachariah. He placed one foot outside the threshold of the entrance door, and as he was bringing the other, Konaduwa, who was angry

---

[1] Text B has left this sentence out.

[2] Interestingly, text B has changed the meaning here to: 'If you refuse, the fetish may kill you.' But in Akan custom, the swearing of an oath involves the one who swears it.

in the last degree, came quickly and took hold of his cloth, and pulled him down, and gave him a sharp slap on the cheek. Owusu was not expecting any brawl, so he got up, shook the dust off his cloth and left the house quietly. Konaduwa followed him with a noisy quarrel, and rained abusive words on him which nearly drowned him.[3]

Owusu's way to his house lay in the front of the house of his second wife, Akua Adae. When she heard the voice of her rival pouring out the abusive words she lent very attentive ears to listen. She heard that the quarrel related to her husband; but as she did not know the cause of the squabble, she hurried to the door and with innocence asked Konaduwa why she was quarrelling and with whom.

"If you wish to side with your husband, I do not mind a button,"[4] said Konaduwa angrily.

The meek Akua Adae, seeing what would ensue, should she retort in the same tone, left the place and went back to her house. As she was going, Konaduwa asked: "Are you going? Have you turned tail, you coward woman?[5] If you are unable to fight, why did you interfere in my case, you ugly, stinking,[6] inquisitive woman?"

---

[3] Text B fails do do justice to this description of a terrified Owusu trying to get away from the scene. We thus have; 'When Owusu heard these words he was astounded. He turned to go and as he did so, Konaduwa, who was furiously angry, seized him by his loin-cloth, dragged him off his feet, and gave him a sharp slap on the cheek.'

[4] 'do not mind a button' (text A), . . . 'do not care a button (text B). Both are inappropriate. Buttons are used in connection with European clothing and thus not in use by the characters involved in this quarrel.

[5] The original has been kept here. The dialogue in the quarrels is so earthy and typically Ghanaian, that it has been attempted to keep Obeng's own choice of words irrespective of how "correct" they are.

[6] Text B has changed these abusive terms to 'hag.'

"Do you say I am a stinking woman? I do not believe my ears," rattled Akua Adae with unbounded passion. Owusu Aduemiri, who stood quite a little distance from the place, ran quickly to the spot for he knew what was to follow, if he did not intervene in time.

Konaduwa replied with all emphasis saying: "I said, nay, I say you are a stinking woman. You are not a true woman, and I do not at all understand why your husband can share his bed with you. If you doubt what I tell you, take me to the Adontenhene's Court, and there you will have to hear something with your own ears."

"I am not as bad and narrow-minded as I think you are," returned Akua Adae, "for if I take any oath or make summons, you would not have a word to say in defence, and the Court Fees will be exacted from our husband; then the money with which he would feed and clothe us and our children will go to the Adontenhene's Treasury Bag. If it were not for this reason, I would let you see that in the flint there is fire, and that if you are as hard as a stone, I am iron which has the strength to break and smash a stone to pieces."

"Foolish Akua Adae!" said her rival, "do not forget what very words you have just spoken against Nana Adontenhene. When you stand before him and his Elders, when the court-criers are shouting 'Hearken, you!' you will then know that in the cannon, there is fire."

When Adae was about to speak, Owusu put his hand round her neck and entreated her to forget all what Konaduwa had said; for he had realised in the last hour, that Konaduwa was not in her right mind. Adae smiled, and said: "I will do all what you tell me, husband."

Owusu said: "Thank you, Akua, one does not love one's wife without reason. Look at my cloth. Konaduwa has torn it to pieces. Look at my forehead, which struck against the frame of her door when she pulled me down, the place has swollen."

Adae then asked her little boy, Kwame Atoapoma, to bring

a lantern. When he came, they found that Owusu's forehead bore a wound from which blood was oozing. Adae then set water on the fire and dressed and bandaged the sore for Owusu.

He was very much pleased, and said: "How true it is that after a great storm, there is always calm." He then bade Adae 'Good-night', and repaired to his house.

CHAPTER 4

A Mother's Yearning

AS OWUSU was going go his house, he met with his mother who had gone to his end in his absence several times that evening; and as she could not guess where he had gone, she was going to Akua Adae's house to inquire if she had seen him. When Odakwaa Aboroma (for that was the name of Owusu's mother) was going to Akua Adae's house, she met with Konaduwa who was very hotly angry. She asked Konaduwa why and with whom she was quarrelling; but she did not receive any answer. She thought Konaduwa was quarrelling with Adae. Odakwaa then turned and looked at Owusu who was being led by his son Atoapoma with a lantern. On seeing the bandage on his head which bore a speck of blood, she exclaimed with horror, saying: "Puei, puei, puei. Aduemiri, you are done for. What gave you this wound. Owusu, do speak to me, I am losing my mind. Are you a living dead?"

Owusu then said: "Mother, keep quiet, let us go home, and I will tell you all about it."

The impatient woman repeatedly asked him to tell her all, there and then; but Owusu did not say a word. The woman then asked the boy if he knew what had caused the wound. With boyish eagerness Atoapoma told his grand-mother that he heard his father telling his mother that Konaduwa knocked him down and that his head struck against a door frame which wounded him. He added that it was his mother who had just dressed the wound and bandaged it. He concluded that Konaduwa started a quarrel with his mother, but she had kept mum.

On hearing this, Odakwaa rushed like an enraged tiger[1] into the house of Konaduwa, and with all possible breath-rending anger, she said: "Do explain to me, you quarrelsome woman, why a woman can hurt her husband so dreadfully. What on earth prompted the quarrel?"

"Ask your son, for he knows what he did. I do not tremble a whit before you and your confederated allies. I am not unaware that you hate me with that hatred which no kindness or presents can appease. You are superlatively ungrateful, and like the grave, you are never satisfied, and so henceforth I will never try to please you, for all the waters of the ocean can never turn the swan's black legs white."[2]

"All right. Customarily, no woman speaks with such impudence to her mother-in-law; and upon this I am going to see that you be divorced."

"Will you marry your son? If your son marries a thousand wives and you disgraced them all in public as you are now disgracing me, you will have to arrange a thousand divorces. But mind you, if you throw a stone at every dog that barks at you, the stones in your street will soon be as precious as jewels."

"I have no heart for all these wiles," said Odakwaa.

"I have no stomach for such affronts either," returned Konaduwa.

"Tell me before the people[3] why you knocked your husband down and tried to dash out his brains."

"I will not utter a word even if you were to put me into a bottle."

---

[1] As there are no tigers in Africa, this is another of Obeng's unfortunate similes, though as mentioned later, it is possible that the author uses the term 'tiger' to refer to another indigenous cat.

[2] Text B has here: ". . . for all the waters of the ocean can never wash the spots from a leopard".

[3] Text A has " . . . before this assemblage." Obeng seems to favour 'hard words' when ordinary ones would be more effective.

The exchange of these words attracted many more people to the scene. Some upbraided Konaduwa; others sympathised with her. Some of the latter asked her to explain the cause of the quarrel with her mother-in-law, so that they could assist in appeasing her anger, should it be found that she was in the wrong. But still she did not like to utter a word, to the amazement of all. Presently, however, she forced herself to speak, and said:

"Harken to me, I pray, all you assembled. It is because of you, but not because of my mother-in-law, that I am speaking. My husband sent me to his farm with a new servant he recently bought. On the farm this servant began to show me signs of love. He beckoned me to go to him, and being ignorant of his intentions, I went there. But he had nothing to tell. This he did more than once. Seeing the evil that was on his mind, I told him that I had no inclination for such follies. At this he tossed his cutlass and caught it in his hands, brandished it in fury, bit his finger and threatened my life. But luckily, before he had time to execute his wishes, the voice of some men passing on the road nearby was heard, and like a hunted stag, he stole away into the bush and left me in the farm. Not knowing whether he had made an ambush on the road, I was compelled to remain in the farm with all fright imaginable. Nobody passed there until about five o'clock; when four men returned from a village, and I fell in with them. On my arrival home, being overcome with wonder and fright, I forgot either to go or to send to greet my husband according to custom. But Owusu was not alarmed by my unusual absence, and did not come to find me until after seven o'clock. And so it was nothing, but this sheer neglect of me that prompted the quarrel." When she said this, thinking that she would be justified, her face beamed with radiant smiles.

When the above statement was being made, Odakwaa walked up and down the street with impatient sighs and steps like a trapped animal in a cage.

Scarcely had the last word left Konaduwa's lips, when she said:

"You have killed Owusu, and you must take the consequences, you quarrelsome woman. Were some other woman to treat your brother in like manner, would you have it?" She then turned to the people, and said: "Save me, you gentlemen assembled. My legs can no longer carry my weight."

On saying this she flung herself down and rolled forwards and backwards like the sea whose waves are set in motion by the winds, and screamed like a jay. Konaduwa looked at her intently, and gathered herself into a black brooding cloud of anger. When she was about to thunder upon her mother-in-law, a gentleman in the crowd requested her to explain the cause of the quarrel there and then so that they could assist in appeasing the intense anger of the woman, should they find she was in the wrong. Still she remained mum. The man then turned to Odakwaa and asked her to exercice patience for their sakes. But she said if Konaduwa had no respect for the men, she should be paid in her own coin. She said she had heard that Konaduwa had sworn that her husband should divorce her, contrary to the customs of the country; therefore in her opinion the case could not be settled outside the Adontenhene's Tribunal.

This statement passed a searchlight of truth and conviction through the minds of the people who assembled there, and they left the place one by one like the men who surrounded and accused the woman who was caught in the act of fornication. Though Konaduwa too was convinced, she became intensely angry, and began to howl and shout and thundered on the men who came there, and said: "My goodness! What ridiculous creatures men are. What cowards too. They are as brave as lions before a horde of savages, but before a woman — *kapok!*"

The remaining men, seeing that she was still pertinacious and obstinate in the last degree, ceased to plead for her; but she being confident of success, shouted all the more with a subtle emphasis of scorn.

CHAPTER 5

The Report

AMONG THE men assembled there, was one whom Odakwa respected. This man held her by the hand, and led her to her house, when Konaduwa was still brawling. Not long after her departure, Kwaku Anyinam, a trusted minister to Nana Addo Kwame, the Adontenhene, happened to pass by on his own accord. When Konaduwa saw him she shouted more loudly, and repeated the words she first spoke to Akua Adae, her rival, at the beginning of the quarrel. She then lay a stronger emphasis on these words:

"You say the Adontenhene and his Elders, including Nana Adoma Hemma, the Queenmother, are all extortioners. You will be answerable sometime to the owners of this town."[1]

When Anyinam heard this, he exclaimed: "Madam Konaduwa, I have found a treasure-trove in your mouth. You say somebody lives in this town who has been so fearlessly able to speak against the Adontenhene whose justice, generosity and affection towards his subjects is known throughout Akyem, Asante, Kotoku, Accra and Akuapem? You say that the same person had the audacity to speaking ill against our gracious and esteemed Queen-Mother as well as the Elders of Abetifi. Why did you not report the case officially to the Linguist, so that sheep might be slaughtered before the news reaches the Elders? You have intentionally concealed

---

[1] Obeng here refers to the unrest that permeated Kwahu society for the first few decades of this century. There was tension between the 'asafo': the educated young men of Kwahu, and the chiefs. The former felt that the chiefs were extorting money from them and wanted to break their traditional predominance. The period 1905 – 1933 experienced 3 destoolments and 3 abdications in the paramountcy of Kwahu.

15

the matter and you have therefore broken the Great Oath of the Omanhene, to whom you will be answerable."

Having said this, Anyinam went to the house of Okyeame Kwadwo Kuma with the speed of a lightning and reported the case to him. No sooner had he finished speaking, when twelve sheep were caught in the street and slaughtered; their prices varied from *Asia*[2] to *Dwaa*.[3] One foreleg of each sheep was put aside for the offender, according to the custom of the country. The Okyeame then went with the dead sheep[4] to the house of the Adontenhene, who, on seeing the carcasses, sent for Adane, the Head Drummer, whom he ordered to sound a summoning call. The big drums, the talking drums and all the smaller ones were beaten with not a little vehemence, and the horns were blown.

The sudden sounding of the drums set the whole town in commotion. Men, women and children who had gone to their farms[5] to do their usual work rushed home, and forced their way to the *Ahenfie* [6] to hear what was the matter. You can imagine what pandemonium ruled the place. Stool-carriers from the houses of the Elders poured in from all the corners of the town, carrying the chairs or stools of their masters.

In his eagerness, the Principal Sword-Bearer, Kwabena Somua, who was then in an extreme hurry, knocked down a young woman carrying some food on a tray. Down went the young woman and the tray, and the bridal food intended for the husband of

---

[2] Twenty-four shillings.

[3] Thirty shillings.

[4] Text A uses the term 'flesh of the sheep'. Text B uses 'carcasses'.

[5] Obeng has obviously got the sequence of events wrong here. It is still late evening and therefore dark, nobody would be in their farms at this hour.

[6] Akan for 'Palace'

another young woman named Afriyie was spilled on the ground and the dishes shattered to pieces.

The young girl rose to her feet, and in fit of anger said to the Sword-Bearer: "Why did you act so foolishly? Have you got your eyes at your anus?"[7]

Among the Akans, the word "FOOL" is never spoken to an ordinary man by any woman whatever. It is punishable by fines and the slaughter of sheep.[8] Unfortunately, Kwabena Somua was not an ordinary man. As stated before, he was the Chief Sword-Bearer who wore a head-gear made of an eagle's feathers with a replica of two sheep horns, one gilded with gold and the other with silver fixed in front of his hat. This hat indicated the loftiness of his rank. As you can imagine, this insult was considered most aggravating. The case was therefore reported to the Gyaasihene who was in charge of all the household of the *Ohene*. Two sheep were at once slaughtered and their fore-legs were sent to Abire, for such was the name of the young woman. Her parents, her husband and Afriyie, who sent her, were informed of what had happened. Afriyie's husband decided that Afriyie should be responsible for the case and pay all expenses which might be incurred, to free Abire from all encumbrances. Afriyie had nothing to do or say but to accept the terms. Considering the seriousness of the case, and how high the expenses might be, Afriyie sulkily left the place to her father's house with the intention to report the case to him. Her father was not in the house, so she asked her younger brother to go round her

---

7   This outburst obviously hurt the sensibilities of the British editor, who changed it to: 'Have you no eyes in your head'.

8   Refer also Peter Sarpong, 'Ghana in Retrospect' p. 92: "For a woman to call a man 'fool' for whatever cause, is unpardonable, no matter the degree of provocation, or difference in age, or degree of relationship. Such behaviour is conceived of as a challenge to an exchange of blows. Yet he should not accept it or he is socially branded as a coward, a fool, a bully — 'a woman fighter'."

father's friends to see if he might be found. He was found in the house of a physician who was attending a nephew of Afriyie's father. The medicine man had prescribed some things which must be procured for the preparation of the medicine. No woman or man other than the nearest relative of the patient was to touch the prescribed things. Afriyie's father was therefore very busily engaged and could not come immediately, as Afriyie expected. Afriyie and her mother were not a little annoyed, and the young woman could not control her anger, so she said:

"Now that I am in hot waters, my father has left me severely alone while he looks after his nephew. Never mind. God is there. I know the Adontenhene will not kill me because of this case; but a fine will be imposed on me. If I bear a child, that will be another servant for my father[9] to be used as his bought slave."

Her father, who had arrived by now and was standing outside to listen to all what was being said in the house, then entered, and with intense anger he said to Afriyie:

"Do you dare speak thus to your father who gave you birth? You have proved yourself ungrateful. You have no respect for me. You are now married, and soon you will be a mother. If after you have troubled yourself about your child until he grows to your present age and he were to speak to you in the same tone as you just spoke to me, would you like it?"

Afriyie was ashamed of what she had said behind her father's back. She fell on her knees and asked his pardon. Her mother and brothers also implored the father to forgive her. The man then calmly explained to them why he could not come at once.

---

[9] The sentence as written by Obeng is ambiguous, it is not clear whether it is the Adontenhene who will get the child in lieu of a fine, or the father, whom she would have to reimburse by giving him her child. The insinuation is that she herself was treated as a slave in her father's house. The intervention of the previous editor has not improved this passage, so we have rewritten Afriyie's outburst to make the meaning clearer.

They all understood, and he readily forgave his daughter.

Afterwards he went to the house of the Mankrado[10] and asked him to intercede in the case and try to bring the charges down. The Mankrado gave him a fair promise, so he and his family were able to eat and to pass a restful night.

------

[10]   An adviser to the chief in the same way as the Krontihene.

CHAPTER 6

The Arrest and Trial of Konaduwa

AFTER THE sheep had been slaughtered and the announcement made to the Adontenhene and his Elders, Anyinam returned to arrest Konaduwa as a prisoner of oath. She was asked to pay the arrest fee of eight shillings; but as she had no money on her, she gave the silver bangle she wore on her left wrist in lieu of the amount. A piece of hollowed pawpaw stem was given to her as a sign of her being a prisoner of oath. This she was ordered to carry with her anywhere she went until the case would be heard and judged. Formerly, the wrist of an oath prisoner was shackled to a heavy log; but when the conditions were ameliorated by the advent of the white man, a hollow pawpaw stem was issued instead.

When the prisoner was brought to court, she was asked to find someone to stand surety for her. She asked her husband to do so. Owusu said he could not do so without any of her relatives. Her maternal uncle and her father came to support Owusu. They were asked to swear that in the event of Konaduwa losing the case, they would readily pay all the expenses without trouble or delay. They swore to do so.

The Tribunal Registrar then stood up, and Adusei Akyakya and the other Court-Criers cried loudly saying: "*Yeretie, yeretie, oo! Aso nto nkom! Odede oo!*" That is: 'Hearken ye. All ears must be quiet as if in sleep. Keep perfect silence, everybody.' Adusei, the Chief of the Court-Criers, wore his cap made of the skins of a white monkey, finished with red baft; his subordinates wore theirs made of the skin of the ordinary black monkey.

After this official bidding of silence, perfect silence deep as death ruled over the Court. The Registrar then held his charge-book in both hands, and loudly and distinctly read the charges against Konaduwa.

State Versus Konaduwa

(i)   "That you, on Saturday, the fifth of July, 1913, at a farm, did say that a certain man attempted rape on you, contrary to the customs of the State, but when you came home, you failed to report the case. Are you guilty or not guilty?"

"Not Guilty."

(ii) "That you, on the same day and place, did say that a certain man attempted to take your life; but when you came home, you did not report it, but by intentional concealment broke the Great Oath of the Omanhene. Are you guilty or not guilty?"

"Not Guilty."

(iii) "That you, on the same date, in the town of Abetifi, and in your house, did swear the Great Oath of the State and enforced it with fetish oath by *Fofie* and *Obonyame* that your husband must divorce you contrary to the customs of the State. What do you plead?"

"Guilty, but with Explanation."

(iv) "That you, in the same day, and in your premises, did charge all the Adontenhene's brave warriors who assembled there with cowardice and compared them with *kapok* which is a very comprehensive insult. What do you plead?"

"Not Guilty."

(v) "That you, on the same day, and in this town did say
that somebody was bold enough to speak ill against
the Adontenhene whom we adore with all possible awe
and reverence; and also against the esteemed Queen-
mother as well as the Elders of this town; but you intentionally concealed it; contrary to the Customs of this
State. Are you guilty or not guilty?"

"Not Guilty."

(vi) "That you on the same day, and in your premises, did
say that your husband has bought a slave contrary to
the British laws. Are you guilty or not guilty?"

"I will be answerable to the British Court, not to you."

The Registrar turned to the Akyeame, and asked them to
tell the Adontenhene and his Elders all what the accused had
said.

The accused was then asked to go into the witness box to
give her evidence. She went; but when she was asked to swear
that she would tell the truth, the whole truth, and nothing but
the truth; she asked with pretentious dignity: "And who is the
plaintiff in this case?"

"The State," Okyeame Safo replied. "We will examine you,
and if we satisfy ourselves that you are innocent, you will be
acquitted; if not, you will be dealt with according to the laws
of the State."

"Right, will any of the Elders here assembled examine me
too?"

"Decidedly," said the Mankrado.

"And will the Adontenhene too exercise his usual power
of ordering one of you to pronounce judgment?"

"Exactly so," said one of the Akyeame.

"And who will retire into consultation before the judgment is given?"

"The Elders, as usual."

The accused then said with blazing audacity: "As it is, I find that I am like a crockroach who has fallen amongst a multitude of fowls.[1] There is nobody in this court who will give ear to my defence, for all of you are interested in the case. I will therefore reserve my defence until fresh people who have no interest in the case sit on it."

A very tumultuous noise arose in the court. Some enthusiasts admired her far-sightedness, and others reproached her for her impenetrable stubbornness. Tortuous and circuitous questions were pelted at her, but she did not say a word.

The Adontenhene who had been silent since the opening of the court, then prepared to speak. Adusei Akyakya and all the Linguists stood up, according to custom, and the court criers shouted for silence, and perfect silence reigned at the premises. Addressing Okyeame Owusu, the Adontenhene said: "Ask Konaduwa by which court she would like her case to be tried?"

She replied that she preferred the District Commissioner's Court.

"Does she not like that the Omanhene tries her?"

"No, Nana."

"Why?"

"Because he is your kinsman; and, besides, in any fine that you collect at the court he has a share."

"Does she mean then that the Omanhene will be biased towards her?"

"Emphatically yes."

Her father and her husband, who stood surety for her became

---

[1] Text B has changed this effective simile to: 'I am a lamb who has fallen amongst wolves'.

sorely afraid; and asked her to retract what she said, else the consequence would be far worse than what they expected. Konaduwa told them that if they had the hearts of rabbits, they should retire.

The Adontenhene then ordered that two sheep should be caught and slaughtered instantly, because of the statement the accused made at the open court against the Omanhene. This having been done, he calmly granted the woman her permission to withdraw the case to the District Commissioner's court as she desired. The forelegs of the sheep were sent to her, and the flesh sent through some Nhenkwaa to the Omanhene Boateng Asabranna.

CHAPTER 7

Before the District Commissioner

WHEN THE assembly broke up, Konaduwa sped quickly away with the intention to go to Asiakwa to report the case to the District Commissioner. But at Anyinam, the Birem had overflown its banks and a ferry-toll of sixpence was exacted by the ferrymen from every passenger. Konaduwa was asked by one of the ferrymen to pay the amount. A smile like eternal sunshine parted her lips and brightened her teeth, which had a gap at the centre of the upper row.

"By Jove," exclaimed the ferry-man, "this woman has exceptionally fine teeth. Madam, keep your sixpence and I will pay it for you."

Konaduwa thanked him with a bow, and tied up her coin in the corner of her handkerchief.

The man then asked some of his friends to assist in putting the woman's luggage aboard the pontoon. The passengers who were to go on the pontoon were too many, so some of them were eager to push past Konaduwa. It began to rain suddenly. The other ferrymen remained in a hut erected on the other bank of the river, thatched with palm leaves. There was a small fire around which they squatted with their hands spread over it to keep themselves warm. As it was still raining, the passengers remained on the far bank, and by shouting they begged the ferrymen to bring the pontoon to take them across.

The toll-collector said that because of the dark and attractive[1]

---

[1]   Text A has the unfortunate choice of 'swarthy' here.

25

woman he would go with the pontoon. He did so, assisted by one of his friends. When they got to the other side of the river, they found that all the people had been soaked to the skin. Konaduwa's teeth were chattering, and she was trembling with acute fever. She was taken by the hand and placed on the pontoon. Her belongings were removed safely, and because of her illness, care was taken that the vessel would not be overloaded. But the other passengers, freezing with cold, rushed aboard, and one man knocked the sick woman's portmanteau into the river. A boy saw the man who did so, and told him audibly that he had 'sunk' somebody's portmanteau. When they landed, it was found that Konaduwa's portmanteau was missing. the boy pointed out the culprit, who admitted the charge and said he did not do so with intention.

The ferryman said that if it did not contain much wealth, the man should buy another one for her; for they could not dive into the river in search of it. But Konaduwa told them that she was involved in a case which might cost her over one hundred pounds, so she was on her way to Asiakwa to request the District Commissioner to either squash the case for her or to minimise the fine. In view of the case, she had obtained a loan of one hundred and fifty pounds, partly in cash and partly in trinkets[2] which she could dispose of for cash if needful. She could therefore not go to Asiakwa without the portmanteau and its valuable contents.

On hearing this, divers jumped into the river in search of it, but all came out again empty-handed. It was sundown, and it was still raining, therefore the men dispersed one by one like people who have come to buy or sell at a market. Konaduwa became infuriated, and though she was ill and cold, she rolled herself hither and thither on the ground and screamed and yelled like a dog who had been frightened, and permitted no conso-lation.

---

[2] Note Obeng's use of the Ghanaian term 'trinket' for gold jewellery. In Text B this has been changed to 'jewels'.

The offender, who had not thought the loss was so great, stood looking at her, and seeing her agony nearly drowned himself. In his apprehension, he stated that a man had hired him for three shillings to go to Dodowa to buy two young sows and a young pig for him. He had received one shilling advance, and the employer gave him fifteen shillings to pay for the pigs. All the money he had on him was sixteen shillings. He paid his ferry fare with sixpence and it remained fifteen shillings and sixpence.

The case was therefore to be taken to the Odekuro of Anyinam, who ordered that both Konaduwa and the man should be sent to Kyebi. The woman insisted upon seeing the District Commissioner first before they reached Kyebi to see the Omanhene of Abuakwa; but the messengers of the Odekuro did not permit this; they therefore went to Kyebi direct.

According to custom, they had to see an Okyeame before going to the Omanhene; they therefore went to the house of Okyeame Aninkora who led them to the Palace. The messengers gave their errand and after a few questions had been thrown to the parties to ascertain the value of the money involved, the Omanhene told them that he had no jurisdiction over a case involving one hundred and fifty pounds, so he asked his Chief-Sword-Bearer to send them to the District Commissioner at Asiakwa. Before they departed, the Omanhene gave them some palm-wine to hold their stomachs. The Anyinam messengers returned to their village, and the Omanhene's man and the two litigants, together with their witnesses, went to Asiakwa.

The Sergeant in charge of the Police Barracks was first greeted, and the Okyenhene's messenger told him his errand. Next Konaduwa was asked to make her statement. She did so. The man who had knocked the portmanteau overboard did the same. The next day, the charge-book was put before the District Commissioner.

The Commissioner inquired whether it was a mere complaint or a summons. Konaduwa said she had no more money on her to make any summons, and entreated the District Com-

missioner to kindly collect her hundred-and-fifty pounds for her.
The District Commissioner again inquired why a woman should
travel with so much money when she was not going to trade
with it.

This gave the woman the chance to narrate her whole story.
She sent for another bag which formed part of her luggage, and
emptied the contents, which were the leg-bones of the many sheep
slaughtered in Kwahu in connection with her case. At this, the
District Commissioner asked her to go home and wait until he
heard from the Omanhene of Kwahu about her case. The Registrar
was asked to draft a letter to the Omanhene of Kwahu asking
for information about one Konaduwa, who had come to him with
the legs of many sheep which she alleged were slaughtered against
'er. The letter was completed and sent to the Asiakwahene for
.nmediate despatch.

The next morning, the District Commissioner came to court
to examine the case of the lost portmanteau. When he had heard
Konaduwa's statement, he asked the man how he could replace
the amount. The man replied that he did not think the woman
had had that amount of money with her, but because the portmanteau was lost she mentioned that amount. He added that
he could not replace it, and the court would have to punish him
in some other way, he would have nothing to say, but to submit
to any punishment. Before the District Commissioner could speak,
the woman became intensely angry, and began to shower abuse
on the man and on the court in general. A constable ordered
"Silence," but then she turned on him and said if he had had
one hundred and fifty pounds which had been lost through another
man's folly, he would not have shouted "Silence, Silence," to
disturb them. The Constable was so annoyed that he reported
the case to the District Commissioner, and threatened to beat the
woman after the Court had risen, for as a woman, she had no
right to charge him with "Fool", according to the established
custom of the Akan.

The woman then said: "Has somebody gone to defecate[3] in your ears? When did I charge you with being a fool, you stupid one?"

The Constable again told the District Commissioner what the woman had said, and he, in turn, ordered that the woman should be charged at once.

Mr. Richard Jones, the Registrar, then conferred with the District Commissioner for a few minutes and then sat down to frame the Charge. This ran as follows:

Rex Versus Konaduwa

"That you on the 14th day of July, 1913, at Asiakwa, did insult and abuse Constable Musa Buzanga during the execution of his duty, thus committing contempt of the King's Court. Are you guilty or not guilty?"

"Is this what the English Court is like?" queried the woman astonishingly. "When a case has not been tried, how can one say one is guilty or not? Even if the case has been tried, how do you expect that one should pronounce one's own judgment against oneself? Tell the District Commissioner that I cannot possibly answer that question."

When he heard this, the District Commissioner said:

"Konaduwa, you are making matters worse. At first you committed contempt of the King's Court, and now you are committing the same misdemeanour towards the King's Judge. Mr. Jones, do frame the second charge, and commit the woman for trial."

The Registrar promptly obeyed, and wrote and read the charge below to the woman.

---

[3] Obeng uses the expression "gone to the stool". *Defecate* is this editor's substitute

Rex Versus Konaduwa

"That you, on the fourteenth day of July, 1913, at Asiakwa, did speak against the established procedure of the British Court and also against the District Commissioner who is the King's Judge. Are you guilty or not guilty?"

"If you ask me this question one hundred times, I will remain mum for as many times. Even if I know that I am guilty, I will never tell you that I am guilty, and ask you to pronounce judgment against me. If I tell you that I am not guilty you would not let me go scot free; but if I say that I am guilty, you will at once pronounce judgement. The Governor sent you here to decide cases before you get your pay, and if you have not fully learnt how to try cases, you should go back to your own country to learn your law properly and also how to judge cases without troubling a woman by asking her '"Are you guilty or not guilty?"'

"This woman is demented,"[4] said the District Commissioner to Mr. Jones.

"I think as that, Sir," replied Mr. Jones.

"If so, she should be sent to Accra for mental examination, and if the Medical Officer thinks it is right, she should be sent to the asylum."

Konaduwa was at once handcuffed and given to the Escort police to march her to Accra.

The man she had accused, who was captivated by Konaduwa's beauty and teeth, and above all by her stammering, approached the District Commissioner and begged him to punish the woman in any other way, and he would bear the punishment for her for he believed that the loss of her property, amounting to one hundred and fifty pounds motivated her stubbornness. The

---

[4]   Text B has here: 'I believe that the accused is of unsound mind'. It will be noticed, that the book has several references to mental imbalance of some kind or the other.

District Commissioner was inclined to agree, but could not revoke his own orders, so off the police went with the prisoner.

When they were a few miles out the town, they met a certain man going into town carrying a pot of palm-wine. One of the constables offered to buy it, and when they had emptied the pot, they went off without paying for it. The owner, on insisting payment, was given a sharp slap that sent him down.

"What?" cried Konaduwa. "Do you policemen act in this way? Did not your master give you some money to pay your way? When the Asantehene's servants were doing the same thing, your master came and took them away. If that was bad why are you doing the same thing?"

"If you don't shut up, I will beat you," said one of the constables.

"You fear to do that," said Konaduwa. "'If you dare, you will see that in the flint there is fire."

The Corporal hushed his friend and said: "The woman is as dangerous as a loaded gun, so be careful, she can charge you and send you to prison."

They did not speak with her again.

Amoako, the ferryman, who was enchanted by the woman, followed them to Accra and to the Principal Medical Officer's office and boldly explained the situation to him. When the doctor examined the woman, he found that she was not mad, but that she had some mental depression which, in his opinion, motivated the impudence of the woman. She was therefore marched back to Asiakwa, and on her arrival, the District Commissioner told her that he would no more try her on the old charges, so he asked the police to withdraw the charges on the ground of "the benefit of doubt . . . " She was then told to go back to her country to be tried by the Elders of her State. She inquired what had become of her lost one hundred and fifty pounds, and the District Commissioner told her that the accused did not believe that she had that amount in the bag but as she insisted on getting it, the Omanhene of Kwahu would be instructed to examine the case.

CHAPTER 8

The Arrest and Trial of Owusu Aduemiri by the District Commissioner for Slave Dealing

THE DISTRICT Commissioner's letter from Asiakwa reached the Omanhene of Kwahu, who replied by sending an explanation of the whole matter, mentioning that Konaduwa had charged her husband Owusu Aduemiri with dealing in the slave-trade, contrary to the British laws; and that he, the Omanhene, had detained Owusu until he would hear from the District Commissioner. The letter was referred to the Sergeant-in-charge, who at once sent a constable and a corporal to Abetifi to arrest Owusu. Instructions were given that Konaduwa, who was the principal witness for the Crown, was to go with the prisoner for prosecution.

When the police arrived, they went to greet the Omanhene, who after giving them food and something to drink, handed the prisoner to them. The witnesses for the prosecution and for the defence were summoned to appear before the corporal to give their statements. Owusu said he would not give any statement until he stood before the magistrate for trial. Akrofi, who was stated to be the person bought, was asked to give his statement; but he too decided to reserve his statement.

Konaduwa, however, stated that her husband told her that he had bought a slave, in the person of Akrofi, for eighteen pounds, and that he gave this man to her to work in her farm. The man attempted to seduce her one day, but she refused. The culprit offered to give her five pounds as hush money, but she did not accept. Instead she came home to report the case to her husband who asked her not to tell anyone about the matter. When Akrofi was questioned, he admitted the charge, and pacified Owusu with another five pounds.

This statement was read over to her two times, and the writer asked whether she wanted to make any alteration, or amend or delete anything which she did not like to embody in the statement. She rather hastily took the pen and made her mark on the paper, before the Omanhene and the assembly. Then the prisoner was brought before the District Commissioner and his charge was read to him as follows.

Rex Versus Owusu Aduemiri

"That you, in Abetifi, in the District of Kwahu in the Eastern Province of the Gold Coast, and within the jurisdiction of this Court, did buy a slave, to wit Obeng-Akrofi, for the sum of £18, contrary to the laws of the Gold Coast.

"Are you guilty or not guilty?"

"Not guilty."

Owusu was then put into the witness-box, and after having sworn to tell the truth, the whole truth and nothing but truth, the Sergeant began to examine him as follows:

"What is your name?"

"Owusu Aduemiri."

"You live in the town of Abetifi?"

"Yes."

"You know the woman in the witness-box?"

"Yes."

"You are related to her?"

"She is not my relative, she is my wife."

"What is her name?"

"Konaduwa."

"You have a farm?"

"Not only one, but many farms."

"Who works in these farms for you?"

"My wives and sometimes myself."

"You remember telling your wife Konaduwa that you bought a slave not many months ago?"

"No."

"Do you know a certain slave called Obeng-Akrofi?"

"I know a certain man called Obeng-Akrofi who is a citizen of Abetifi, but not a slave."

"Do you know anything about that man?"

"A lot."

"Tell this Court all what you know about the man."

"Shall I begin from the time when he was a boy up to this time?"

"No, we want to know how you managed to buy him."

"I have not bought him."

"Does he work in your farm?"

"He does."

"Do you pay him each time he works for you, and if so how much?"

"I do not pay him for his services."

"Explain to the court the reason why you do not pay him for his services, though you say he is not your bought slave."

"That man is in court here, and I think you had better ask him. He is a witness for the crown in this very case."

"Exactly, but you have to give your own evidence before he comes to bear witness for or against you."

"What I know of Obeng-Akrofi recently is this: Not very long ago, he came to buy a cutlass from me at the price of one shilling and sixpence or 'eighteenpence'. He promised to pay for it at a stated time. The time elapsed without payment; and when I demanded it, he came to me with a friend of his, and he offered himself as a pledge for the amount until when he would be able to pay. I told him before the witness that British Laws forbade this, so I could not agree. He then told me there that until the debt was paid, he would voluntarily work in my farm for me. He went to my farm but once, and with this my wife in the Box. Towards the evening, he came home to greet me, and ate the food I had left for him, and then went back to his house. Later when my wife did not come to greet me, I went to her house to see why she kept so long on the farm that day. She quarrelled with me and knocked me down, and when I got up and was rushing out of her house, I struck my head against the door frame. My other wife, her rival, dressed the wound for me. Konaduwa then quarrelled with my mother and my other wife, her rival. This was the beginning of a succession of cases which brought her before Your Worship recently at Asiakwa. This is all I know."

The Sergeant then asked Konaduwa if she had any question to ask Owusu.

"A lot," she said. "Ask him why he fears the white man. Is it because of his pale face or because of his eyes which are like those of a cat?"[1]

"This has nothing to do with the case," interrupted the District Commissioner.

"If you will not allow him to answer this question, then I will ask no more questions," replied the angry woman.

"Do ask questions which have a connection with this case, and which will enable us to find the truth in it."

"Ask him that when I went to the farm with that man, did he send me any food?"

"Do not waste my precious time, woman," said the District Commissioner.

"If you have no time, why do you say you will settle cases? You are not cultivating or trading for the Government, but you receive a very fat pay each month. Perhaps your pay is much bigger than what you father gets in your country. You only go

---

[1] Obeng uses Konaduwa, as a woman, to insult the colonial administration; this is a salient feature of the novel.

to sit at your Office for a long time, and you come to court to ask one or two questions, and go back to eat and then sleep, yet you get your pay. If I want to ask a thousand questions, you cannot hush me."

The Magistrate put down his pen, and snapped his fingers.

"You are not paid for this," said the woman, "so go on to try the case."

"You told the police your husband had bought a slave at Abetifi?"

"Yes."

"For how much?"

"Does not the police know book?"[2] she retorted. "If he is literate, why did he not write all what I told him at Abetifi?"

"He wrote all what you told him at Abetifi."

"All right."

"Tell the Court at what price your husband bought the slave."

"At the price which the police heard me say at Abetifi."

"Look here, woman, have you come to play here again?"

"No one is drumming; how can I play?"

"Your Worship," said the Sergeant, "let us leave this woman alone, and hear the evidence of Obeng-Akrofi."

"Good. Bring him before the court."

"Obeng-Akrofi, Obeng-Akrofi!", the police shouted repeatedly.

Akrofi appeared quickly, and having been sworn, he was put into the Box.

"What is your name?"

"Akrofi."

"Akrofi or Obeng-Akrofi?"

"Obeng Akrofi is my name."

"You live in Abetifi?"

---

²   Text A has (cannot the police read) in brackets.

"Yes."

"You are a farmer?"

"I have only one small farm."

"You are a servant to Owusu Aduemiri?"

"I am a friend to him."

"Do you work in his farms?"

"I have done so only once."

"How much did he pay that day?"

"He paid me with love and kindness."

"How?"

"I had nothing, but one dog whose name is 'Poor-no-Friend'. I then made up my mind to marry; but I had no money, so I decided to make a farm.[3] I had no money and could not even buy a cutlass, and so I went to this man, Owusu, and he gave me one at eighteenpence on credit, and I asked for two weeks to pay for it. I could not pay at the end of the time fixed. I went to ask him to extend the time of payment; but he insisted on having his money. I then offered myself as a pledge, but he said the white man's law forbade that. I therefore volunteered to work in his farm for two days in the week; but I went to his farm but once, because this whole affair came, and since then I have not gone to his farm again."

"Do you still owe him?"

"I have since paid him the amount due."

"Owusu, have you received your eighteenpence?"

"Yes, long ago."

"Why did you not tell the court that you had received your money?"

"Because the court did not ask me."

"When Akrofi offered himself as a pledge, and you refused it, was anyone else there?" asked the magistrate.

"My wife Konaduwa was there."

---

[3] Text B has 'I decided to set up as a farmer', but 'to make a farm' is a very different concept.

"Did Konaduwa hear the amount involved was eighteenpence?"

"She did."

"Akrofi, is this truth?"

"It is true."

"How will you prove that the amount involved was eighteenpence but not eighteen pounds?"

"The day I went to farm with her, she asked me to go and eat, and when I delayed, she said she wondered why I was working until my back would break for the sake of eighteenpence."

"Aha! Did you say so, Konaduwa?"

"Yes."

"You knew that Obeng-Akrofi owed your husband only eighteenpence and not eighteen pounds?"

"Yes."

"Sergeant, then there is no case," said the Magistrate. "Send them back to the Omanhene of Kwahu, and ask him to punish this woman for having falsely accused her husband."

"I never knew that you did not know how to try cases. In my town, when two men get a case, they all make their statements. Then the Elders question them, and fix a point which is to be proved by the witnesses; but there is nothing of this sort at this court. I prefer to go back to be tried by the Elders of my State."[4]

------

[4] As a pensioner, Obeng worked as a translator at the District Commissioner's court at Mpraeso and knew many a good story to tell from his experiences there.

CHAPTER 9

The Transfer of Owusu's Case to the Omanhene of Kwahu Konaduwa Divorced

KONADUWA HAVING said this, the Court rose, and the District Commissioner drafted the following letter and gave it to his Correspondence Clerk for typing.

Ref. No. 47/B.B./Case 78/13

> District Commissioner's Office
> Asiakwa, Birim District.
> 7 August, 1913.

My Good Friend,

I have the honour to inform you that I have examined Owusu Aduemiri under the Charge of "Dealing in the Slave Trade", I have examined Owusu Aduemiri, together with the witnesses for and against the Prosecution, and found that Obeng-Akrofi, the man alleged to have been sold and bought, did voluntarily work for Owusu but once on account of the paltry sum of One shilling and Sixpence, an amount which cannot possibly buy a fowl of fairly good size. Owusu's wife who was the principal witness for the prosecution, now gave evidence that Obeng-Akrofi owed her husband the amount mentioned above, but not £18 as she told the police before you. This being the case, the Court found that there is no case in the matter, and Owusu has consequently been released form the Charge.

I am, however, sending Konaduwa, who coined this sham

criminal charge, back to you, with a suggestion that you either punish or strongly reprimand her as a warning to other people not to act in like manner.

> I have the honour to be,
> Your good friend,
>
> N. N.
>
> DISTRICT COMMISSIONER
> Birim District

At the completion of the above letter, Owusu and all the other people were sent back with the official letter. When they came to the river Birim, which had flooded its banks, Konaduwa saw her old friend Amoako, the ferry-man, and whispered into his ears that Owusu's relatives had openly said that they would dissolve their marriage; and if he liked to marry her, as evidenced in his movements and acts, he should proceed to Abetifi in due course to see how the matter would end. On hearing this, Amoako became as happy as Adam before God took away his best rib, and was full of laughter and sparkling with animation like a child leaving school for holidays. He therefore promised to follow her as soon as possible. Konaduwa warned him, however, to act wisely, for if he did anything to betray his intention, Owusu could customarily swear an oath to preclude him from that marriage, and then all his time and energy spent on her would be wasted for nothing. Amoako nodded to assent to this, and untied two florins from the edge of his handkerchief which he had wished to give her. Astutely Konaduwa refused the offer, and explained that if Owusu divorced her, she would according to custom, swear a fetish-oath upon which she had to confess everything she had done contrary to marriage-custom, and mention any tiny present another man had given her, even if the giver were her husband's relative. If she intentionally or through oversight left anything in secrecy, the fetish would kill her. It was obvious that she must mention that money he intended to give her, and if they married afterwards, he would be charged with seduction and fined heavily, and at last their marriage would be annulled.

When this conversation was going on between them, Konaduwa used to look askance at her husband. Owusu's eyes met with hers accidentally, and he wondered what that shrewd woman was telling the stranger.

The passengers and their luggage were put on the pontoon, and Amoako and his fellow pontoonniers ferried them to the other bank with all hilarity. All the time Owusu was wondering what the conversation between his wife and that Akyem man was about; but he dared not ask her, for he knew full well that she would not tell him the truth, yet it would forewarn her that he was suspicious.

They arrived at Abetifi three days after their departure from Asiakwa, for the whole length of the road was muddy, ankle-deep. O, those old days, when heavy loads weighing sixty pounds were carried on the head through those muddy roads. There was not the least idea of railways and the travelling in ease and comfort as it is now!

On their arrival in Abetifi, the District Commissioner's letter was handed to Okyeame Asabere, one of the eloquent spokesmen, who carried it to the Omanhene. Immediately the *Botom*, the Omanhene's summon drum was beaten, and all the courtiers set out for the Odwenase Street. Luckily the Omanhene had previously invited all the wing-chiefs together with their subordinate chiefs and headmen to meet at Abetifi to discuss a matter relating to their boundary with one of the neighbouring Amanhene.

When they were seated Asabere was asked to bring that letter. When they were contemplating who would read it to them, they saw Teacher Gyesaw passing, dressed fully. All the potentates sat under various glittering umbrellas of multi-colours, with gold-gilded tops, all proverbial. Mr. Gyesaw was sent for, and he quickly came. The letter, which had been sealed with wax, was given to him with a request to read it to the assemblage. He quickly tore the letter open, not knowing that it came from the District Commissioner. From his pocket he pulled his specs, which he cleaned with a handkerchief, and placed on the bridge of his nose. Undoubtedly the letter was written in English; but alas! Gyesaw was an Evangelist who had not reached any Standard class at school. The whole of his training at school was up to the present Infants Class III, so he was only able to read and write Twi. His work as an Evangelist did not warrant any knowledge of English; and so long as he could read Twi and write it he was quite eligible for that evangelical work. He was therefore addressed as "Teacher Gyesaw" as all the other teachers who had been trained through all the schools and in the Theological Seminary. As he was so addressed, it was universally believed that he could read every letter as the others did.

Gyesaw stood at the centre of the large assembly and looked over the letter again and again, the various court-criers of the various chiefs chanting their melodious order of: *"Odede O! Aso nto nkom!"* Gyesaw began to perspire freely, and with the handkerchief he mopped his brow until it became very wet. The Adontenhene then ordered that one state-umbrella should be put over him. He removed his specs, and cleaned them once more, and then cleared his throat. At this the court-criers cried the more, and the place became as silent as the grave.

Gyesaw then said that when he was coming to the assemblage, he saw some men dividing some meat at the Okyenase Street so he wanted to go there quickly to see if he could obtain a share, for because of meat he fasted the previous day. On saying this, the kind Adontenhene ordered his pantry-warder to send a leg of a buffalo and another of a wild hog to Mrs. Gyesaw to cook for her husband. They then entreated him to proceed to read the letter, for as it came from the District Commissioner they did not know whether it carried an order or it demanded an immediate reply.

Gyesaw looked over the letter again and turned the other side, and laughed. He then folded and enveloped it, and put in into his pocket, and asked them permission to retire for ten minutes to ease himself before he come back to read the letter to them. Some of the chiefs and some of the *Nhenkwaa*[1] who were waiting with their itchy ears to hear the contents of the letter were unwilling to let him leave the assembly until the letter had been read through, and some of them attempted to handle him roughly. The Omanhene, however, ruled that he should go and come back in twenty minutes. The Adontenhene interrupted, that if go he should, he must leave the letter behind to enable them to find another clerk to read it to them. To this Gyesaw did not agree; so off he went with the letter. With the haste of an eagle robbed of her eaglets, Gyesaw climbed the hill to the Basel Mission Station where there were two young students from the Akropong Theological Seminary, home for holidays. He met the students taking their breakfast.

"Good appetite," he yelled.

"Good appetite, Sir," the students replied.

"Oh, Are you now having your meal?"

"Yes, Sir," they chorused.

"Then I shall have to wait for a while," said Gyesaw, panting.

"Would you like any of us to do anything for you, Sir?" asked one of the students.

"Oh, Yes! I have been given an interesting letter to read, and because of its exciting contents I have decided to show it to you to read it too."

"Thank you, Sir," said the senior student. He then put down the knife and the fork, and received the letter. He pulled it out of the envelope, and quickly glanced his sharp eyes over it. When doing so, the younger student joined him and both

---

[1] Servants of the Palace

of them read the letter together. The older student then inquired from Mr. Gyesaw if he had already read out the letter to the Omanhene. He answered in the affirmative. He added that if he had not read it, they would not have allowed him to come to the Station with the letter.

"Exactly so," the younger student said. They put the letter into the envelope, and gave it to Mr. Gyesaw.

"And what does the letter say?" inquired Mr. Gyesaw.

"You have read it already, and you know what it says," said the junior student.

"Yes, but I want to see if you understood it in the same way as I did."

"Well, both of us read it together, and none of us asked the other to tell him what it meant."

"You see, you are still in the college, and your minds and intelligence must be fresher than mine, so, I pray, tell me exactly what the letter demands." said Gyesaw earnestly.

Just at this time Kwaku Amenaku came there, panting as the hare.

"Mr. Gyesaw, why do you act in this manner?" he asked.

"You have left the Omanhene and all his chiefs in the scorching sun and come here either to eat or to chat. If you cannot read the letter, tell me and I will go to your wife for the two legs of venison which the Adontenhene gave you."

"Oh, be careful with your tongue. Do not tell tales," Gyesaw said with anger.

One of the students asked Amenaku why he said that; and he narrated the whole story to them; this revealed to them why Gyesaw had wanted them to tell him exactly the contents of the letter. They then asked Amenaku to go back, and promised to accompany Gyesaw to the court in two minutes. He went. The students read the letter once more, and the junior translated it verbatim into Twi on a piece of paper; which he gave to him. Seeing that victory had smiled upon his arms, he flew to the great assembly with the swiftness of a swallow. Before he left them, he faithfully promised to share with them equally anything he would get for the reading of that letter.

Clutching his prize, he went to stand under the canopy of the state-umbrella once more. The court-criers ordered silence. Gyesaw looked about him with a smile on his face, and as custom required, he called Okyeame Asabere, and asked him to listen to what he was going to read for the information of his master. He pulled the letter again from his pocket, and having placed the Twi translation over the original one written by the District Commissioner, he polished his spectacles once more, and loudly and with all possible emphasis he read the translation accurately to the audience.

The acclamations and ovations they all loaded on Gyesaw's small neck, he could not carry. Some said he should be carried in a palanquin; others said in a sedan-chair, to his house. The Omanhene instructed Kwaku Sampa, his Assistant Treasurer to give *Asuaanu*[2] and a hamper of fish which Ko-Boaten had sent in.

When Amenaku was returning from the Mission Station where he saw Gyesaw with the Akropong students, one of his wives detained him regarding some quarrel which his other wife was about to bring. He therefore went to her house to appease and suppress it. From there he went to the public latrine to ease himself.[3] Therefore when he reached the Court, the letter had been read, and the presents and acclamations already given to Gyesaw. He then told the people that it was the Akropong students who had read and translated the letter into Twi for Gyesaw; for they all knew that he could not distinguish A from B, and so he did not deserve the honour given him. But it was too late. Gyesaw had left with his prize, and gone to his house at the Mission Station. Being unsatisfied, Amenaku followed him to

---

[2]   Four pounds.

[3]   This sentence is not found in Text B

the Mission Station, and told the students of the money and fish which Gyesaw had received for the reading of the letter, and urged them to claim their full share. Whether impelled by honesty or by the fact that Amenaku had revealed all to the students, Gyesaw brought the whole prize, money and meat to them, and in dividing it, he gave them the lion's share.

The sun then was at its zenith, much time having been spent by teacher Gyesaw in reading the letter. The Omanhene, therefore, adjourned the court for lunch, and asked them to resume at three o'clock to try Konaduwa for having falsely accused her husband of domestic slavery.

At two o'clock in the afternoon the drums began to beat, and precisely at half past two the court was full to its utmost capacity. The Omanhene who had been bedecked with ornaments, was marched to the court like a little child learning how to walk. His arms were laden with gold trinkets from elbow to the wrist; and he wore a heavy ring on each of his ten fingers; his feet were shod in gold sandals; gold charms and amulets hung from arms and legs: some from the top of the calves to the ankles. Solid gold necklets and chains hung around his neck, and one chain with large links was slung from the right shoulder across the body to the left hip like a sash. On his head was a very heavy gold crown with ferns and feathers that stirred in the wind. His hands and arms were supported, and eagle-eyed attendants, carefully watched his every footstep lest any of the royal decorations should be lost. In front of him all his regalia and paraphernalia was displayed, and he walked slowly but majestically, his retainers holding his waist and supporting him as if he was going to fall at every step. The agile sword-bearers with their gilded swords ran to and fro in front of him with all nimbleness like bees seeking their hive. The court-criers, with their gold-plated caps on their heads, and their cloths lowered to the elbows of the left arms were there; as were the 'soul-washers' with their breast-plates, well polished, suspended round their necks by woven pineapple fibres, glittering like stars. A long string of stool-carriers ran at the immediate front of him, the chief of whom bore the 'Bell-Stool' on his bare shoulders; all of them wore their cloths at their waists. The Bell-Stool had one gold bell at one end and a silver bell at the other. They were suspended at the end of long strips of leather, and lay in the right hand of the bearer who shook them backwards and forwards to let them give their tingling music. The switchers, or elephant-tail carriers, waved gold and silver whisks. Every one of these servants had his cloth at the waist. All these walked or rather crept slowly in front of the Omanhene. Behind him was the *Apirede*, the Dance of the Ghosts, captured by an ancient stool-hunter. Then the big drums, the talking drums and several minor others followed. Then came the Queen-Mother in her sedan-chair, carried by eight strong men, with a large silken fan as her canopy, for women are not entitled to state-umbrellas. The large horns, seven in number, were blowing, and after them all came the Kyidomhene with his retinue, drums and horns.

The pandemonium that ruled over the scene was neither describable nor comprehensible. Amid the din, the Omanhene crept on and on, like a snail on the wall, until they neared the assembly. As soon as they caught sight of him, Amenaku, the Chief Palanquin-Carrier shouted with the voice of thunder, saying: "Arise ye!" With lightning speed, all assembled sprang as one man, to their feet, and kept standing until His Majesty was seated.

When he had taken his seat, Oboe, one of the executioners, snatched his knife from its sheath, put on his leopard cap, tied his cloth at his waist, and with his left hand on his breast, and the right holding the knife, jumped into the assemblage, a tigerish gleam to his eyes. He pointed the knife at the Omanhene and began to sing his praises. In the course of this, the brave deeds done by his predecessor on the stool were enumerated — wars and battles won by them; the enemies they put to flight; those they conquered, captured, tortured and slew — all was repeated in the praise-songs. At the end of this the horns blew; the tom-tom, the talking drums and all the other drums jointly sounded their homage to the monarch. Just when the noise subsided, Yaw Donko, the other executioner, who was more eloquent and much smarter than Oboe, and who had dressed in the same uniform, stood forth and commenced another song in praise of the remaining deeds of the ancient kings. At the end, the horns and the drums sounded again. Then the court-criers demanded silence, and a hush fell.

Okyeame Asabere, the Acting Head of the Linguists, then stood up and said:

"Wing Chiefs, Sub-Chiefs, Headmen and everybody, hearken ye! His Majesty the King, the All-powerful, the Lion on the plains, the Leopard in forests, the huge and fearsome Snake in the fields, and our most gracious and kindly King, has ordered me to tell you that we have met here this afternoon to decide a case which has been transferred to him from the District Commissioner's court at Asiakwa, and he solicits your kind assistance and sound judgment!"

After saying this, he asked Konaduwa to stand up at the midst of the assembly. She went there with her headkerchief still tied around her head. This was at once removed from off her head and thrown away by a servant. Konaduwa told that servant that he must look after the headkerchief carefully, for she had a gold nugget tied into one corner of it. They hushed her and asked her to mention who was standing surety for her in order to pay all costs of she were found guilty. She said that she had no such person, so the prison would have to stand surety for her, which meant that in the event of her losing the case, she should be jailed.

The linguist then told her that she had charged her husband with buying a slave, and the case had been brought before the District Commissioner at Asiakwa, who had sent it back to them for investigation. The District Commissioner informed them in his letter that they should punish her. Because of that they had met there, and if she had something to say which might mitigate her punishment, she should speak.

Konaduwa asked permission to ask one question and when it was granted, she asked:

"Is it because of a case between a wife and her husband that all the Kwahu chiefs and potentates have met here to-day? The proverb is too true — 'Every knife is out when the bull is down!' If I were not a woman, I would tell you that you have time to spend, no, to waste. A case which the District Commissioner could not settle, who else has power here to settle it and punish me? If I should have been punished, why did not the District Commissioner see to it? Let me ask you this, or remind you, or awaken you, if you are sleeping. In the olden times when our ancestors judged their high cases in Kumasi, was any case returned from there to be judged by you so that you could inflict punishment? Answer me this! If not, why do you want to cheat me because I am a woman? I will make no defence, and if you can judge the case and punish me when I have not spoken, be sure that there is a court which is much higher than this, to which I will appeal. You don't seem to have heard of me. I outmatched the District Commissioner at Asiakwa. He sent me to Accra in hand-cuffs, but I came back scot free, because the sword of the law and justice is double-edged. The law is no respecter of persons. I am a masculine woman, and if you like try me! I warn you it is dangerous to play with fire."

The Nifahene sat quietly, nodding his head, and then said:

"If I had one woman in my town who is as strong as this woman, I would ask permission to banish her from my Division."

"If all the women in your Division are so foolish as to take anything without reasoning," she retorted, "the Abetifi women are not so!"

On hearing this, the Benkumhene said:

"Linguists of the State, hear me for the information of your masters. I am the King of the Left Wing of this State. All and everybody knows that every dirty and nasty thing we do with the left hand, and as I am the King of this Wing, I know that I am the King of all nonsense and foolish things. This much I admit. But permit me to say one or two things."

"Speak on," the Linguists responded.

"I will most humbly crave the permission of the other Wing-Chiefs and that of His Majesty, the King, to ask permission to retire for consultation before we proceed any further into the case before us."

The Omanhene readily granted permission and added that the Chiefs of the Right and Left Wings should go out for consultation, promising that anything they would decide and tell him, he would abide by.

The two Wing-Chiefs and about ten of their Sub-Chiefs and their Headmen then walked off to Kwakwa-Gyeduase, and under the canopy of that large shade tree, they sat down. The Benkumhene then stood up and said:

"My colleagues, I hope you all will agree with me that we must learn something from the merest trifles, and that observation is the best teacher. From all what I have seen and heard from the woman whose case we are about, I adduce that she is shrewd and cunning and at the same time an enticing bird; if we follow her we shall reach nowhere, and the case will never end. But I see that our master does not see this, for the camel never can see his hump. I have heard that this same woman has a series of cases pending in the courts of the Adontenhene and the Omanhene, but it appears that she does not care a dime for anyone. You heard her say that she even outmatched the District Commissioner. She is, as far as I see, practically invincible, and though you, my superiors of the Right-Wing have not yet spoken, my suggestion is that we humbly lie prostrate before the Omanhene and the Adontenhene, and pray them to agree that the Omanhene squash this case under his heavy sandals. If there be any slaughtering of sheep, or any fine, we shall share, and set the woman scot free. If you think there is any wisdom in what I have said, so be it; if you think it is folly, let my statement come back to my mouth."

When he sat down, the Nifahene said:

"I know that small beginnings often have great endings. If we make light of this case, who knows what the prattling tongue of this masculine Abetifi woman will say later. She may say worse things that might affect or tarnish our beloved and esteemed Omanhene or the Adontenhene, his cousin, who are our masters. I therefore do agree with you."

All the other Sub-Chiefs and the Headmen concurred and whole-heartedly supported the statements of the two Wing-Chiefs; not because of their rank, but because they found that there was much wisdom in what they had said. Having appointed the Mpraesohene to be their spokesman, they prepared to rejoin the court. Before they left their place of consultation, another chief said:

"But suppose those in authority reject the proposal we have made, how shall we save the situation?"

The Benkumhene said, "Though they are our masters, they cannot possibly do anything without our concurrence and support. They are like the trunk of the body, and we are the extremities. We feed and clothe and wash them. If they throw us away, they would be nothing. Besides, the Omanhene promised openly that he would abide by anything we would have decided, sɔ I have every confidence that the case will end amicably, for you all know that the Omanhene is not at all changeable."

When they were thus communing, a sword-bearer was sent to tell them that they had kept the Omanhene and other people waiting longer than was expected. They therefore hastily came back and resumed their seats. The Mpraesohene then stood up and said:

"Linguists assembled, pray listen to me. My Lords, His Majesty graciously granted us permission to retire for consultation about the case of Madam Konaduwa. When we went we could not easily find the proverbial 'Old Woman.' She had been very busy with some other people who were consulting her. That was why we inevitably kept you sitting for such a long time, and for which we have to humbly apologise. When we got the

'Old Woman,' we put our case before her, and after a fairly long meditation, she told us that, pardon me to say, my lords, the whole case, from its commencement to its present stage, is entirely a foolish case, for it is a marriage case, arising from nothing but sheer jealousy. But My Lords, you all agree with me that jealousy, like hunger, assails every man and woman. Considering this in view of what the 'Old Woman' advised us to most humbly tell you for the information of our masters, the Omanhene and his noble cousin, that the Omanhene may stamp the whole case out under his heavy sandals, we advise the Omanene to dismiss the case."

There was dead silence. The speaker obtained permission to sit down.

The Omanhene and the Adontenhene then conferred together, and then called the Kyidomhene to stand in front of them, and then after a short but pithy conversation, the Adontehene asked the Linguists to listen. They all, about three dozen of them, stood up as one man. Then the court-criers shouted at the top of their voices: *"Odede oo, Yetie oo Aso nto nkom!"* The Adontenhene then said:

"Tell our Wing-Chiefs that we thank them heartily for the good advice they have brought us from the proverbial 'Old Woman.' The Omanhene and myself have considered the case in the same light when they were away, and we have decided to abide, as we promised before, by what they have told us. Therefore tell Konaduwa that she is now free; no, wait a minute. She told that servant who removed her headkerchief that she had a nugget at the edge of it. Ask her whether that statement was correct or whether she made it because she was frightened. If she reallv had a gold nugget, it means that she has money enough to meet every expense in connection with this case."

Konaduwa said: "Okyeame, you see I was fishing in troubled waters, and that was why I said what I said. I pray, let Nana finish his statement before I tell him which is which."

"Tell her," said the Kyidomhene, "a chicken is not wiser

than the hen! She must say whether what she said was correct or not. If she tells a lie, she is still in our grip."

"I am not at all afraid," she asserted. "For the barking of a dog does not hurt the clouds. I am like an egg in the midst of black ants. They can only walk around me, but can by no means injure me. Do not arouse my passion, but let me answer what the Adontehene asked me."

The Adontenhene again emphatically said:

"I hold the keys of every case in this State, and whatever advice I give the Omanhene, he will take it. Tell us the truth. Had you any nugget in the corner of your headkerchief or not?"

"Er, er, I bought that headkerchief for twenty shillings," she stammered, "and because it was so roughly handled and screwed up in the hands of that servant, I said so. I cannot tell a lie before you, Nana."

"Therefore she had no nugget there?"

"I had none, Nana, and I lie prostrate before you, begging for mercy."

"I am glad to hear you telling the truth at last; and since repentance is next to innocence, I tell you that in the name of His Majesty, the King, I release you and dismiss the case on which we have sat up to now. But if you have any other case pending for hearing apart from the present one, we shall try it hereafter, unless you adopt some other means and change your conduct so as to arouse our sympathy and mercy. In the meantime, you are hereby severely reprimanded for daring to lay a false charge. If you or any other person does so again, the offense will be severely dealt with according to our native laws and customs. If a woman can act in such a manner, she undoubtedly disgraces our womenfolk in this State and this renders them repulsive to our men for marriage or even concubinage."[4]

---

[4] Text B has omitted this reference to *concubinage*, but since Obeng, for whatever reason, decided to keep this in the text, so has the present editor.

Konaduwa knelt down and humbly thanked the authorities for having freed her from that charge — which, in her opinion, was the heaviest of all the charges brought against her.

The Omanhene then asked the Linguists to announce to the court that they had sat for too long, so they must go home to rest; but the court would resume at eight o'clock the following morning.

After the assembly had dispersed, Owusu went to his father-in-law and told him that he received his daughter Konaduwa from him in marriage, but as she nearly got him jailed through her unjustified jealousy, he had therefore come to give her back to him and to dissolve the marriage from that very hour. All the presents he gave her during their marriage, she was free to keep, he would not claim any. She was free from the swearing of the usual fetish oath. Her head-money, or dowry, which was thirty pounds, he would forego, and he would take charge of all the children they had. He would also allow her to fetch foodstuffs from her farm until when she would be married again.

Six bottles of gin and a castrated fat sheep were brought in by Konaduwa's father to thank Owusu for his unbounded generosity. These gifts symbolised the seal of the transaction and all what Owusu presented. He had no further claims on Konaduwa and her family.

CHAPTER 10

The Trial of Akrofi

THE ADONTENHENE'S police brought Akrofi in hand-cuffs the following morning and committed him for trial. The charges against him were read as following:

> (i) "That you, on Saturday, the fifth of July, 1913, at a farm, did attempt to commit rape on Konaduwa, Owusu Aduemiri's ex-wife, contrary to the Customs of this State. Are you guilty or not guilty?"
>
> "Not guilty."
>
> (ii) "That you, on the same date and at the same place did threaten to take Konaduwa's life by tossing your cutlass in the air and brandishing it at her. Are you guilty of not guilty?"
>
> "Not guilty"

Just after this, the Pitikohene asked the Nifahene to beg the Omanhene to adjourn the court for about half-an-hour, more or less; for he had something to suggest before the trial began. The Omanhene, accordingly, adjourned the court and the chiefs repaired to Kwaku Boadua's house. There the Pitikohene addressed them saying:

"My Lords, I have heard that the same charges brought against Konaduwa are now brought against Akrofi, but with a slight variation, since she did report the crimes when they were committed. In my opinion, both Konaduwa and Akrofi must be tried together as co-defendants, and the charges be amended thus: **The State versus Akrofi and Konaduwa.** If they lose the

55

case, they will be punished together; and thus our time will be saved."

The Sadanhene, having obtained permission to speak, retorted saying:

"I do not at all fall in with the last speaker; for it appears that Konaduwa is the principal witness for the prosecution in both charges. It was she who reported that Akrofi attempted to seduce her, and when she resisted he threatened to take her life. If both are tried as co-defendants, — who will be the witness for the prosecution? — for nobody was with them at the farm. This being the case, how can they be joined together and tried as co-defendants?"

Another man said: "Konaduwa need not make any statement at all, for as soon as Akrofi loses the case, she too will be guilty of her charge — the breaking of the Great Oath of the State by concealment."

It was therefore decided that Akrofi should be tried alone, and Konaduwa would be signing her own death-warrant, if she gave evidence against him.

Half an hour passed quietly and the court resumed. Akrofi was put into the witness-box for his defence. He was sworn and asked to mention his surety. He said 'Prison' should secure him. He was then asked to make his statement. He began:

"My name is Akrofi. I live in Abetifi. I am a poor man. I have no living relative besides my only aunt who is now very old and feeble. My only property on earth is my small dog 'Poor-no-Friend'. I wanted to marry, but I had nobody to help me. I went to buy a cutlass from Owusu on credit, and promised to pay for it after two weeks. The time passed without payment of the debt. When Owusu demanded payment, I could not honour his bill. I therefore volunteered to work for him in his farm. The first and the only day I went to him for orders, he asked me to accompany his wife Konaduwa to her farm. At the farm, seeing that I worked hard, the woman mocked me, and at the end charged me to be fuzzy and pigheaded, contrary to the customs of the Akans. But as poverty knows no law or alternative, I held my peace. She then said she was afraid I would tell her husband all what she told me at the farm. So, in order to find a pretext to protect herself, she began to coin charges and said I wished to beat her; and if I dare she would charge me with assault and hand me over to the police. When I found that she wished to put me into trouble, I bade her good-bye and came home. When I arrived home, I did not report the incidents to her husband. If this were not all that happened at the farm, and I made any attempt to seduce the woman, I swear the Great Oath of the State, and may *Fofie* and *Obonyame* and *Pra* terminate my life in less than forty days. If the woman is able to come forward to respond to these oaths, then I will resign everything to the fetishes and calmly bear the brunt of the case."

Konaduwa was then asked by one of the akyeame if she could respond to the oaths. She said her husband would benefit from the case by exacting pacification or adultery fees, but as they were now separated, she would no more argue. It was, however, pointed out to her that the court did not sit because of the damages due to Owusu, but because of the concealment of the crime. So if she knew fully well that Akrofi really did what she stated, she must either respond to the oaths or else apologise.

"The case which happened at first you have not been able to settle, why do you want to bring in another?" she queried.

"Never mind, "one of the chiefs retorted. "Akrofi has now broken the egg, and it is for you to deal with the yolk. Can you respond to the oaths or not?"

"Before I say anything, please permit me to ask a few questions."

"We are not going to try you according to the English system by allowing both parties to ask a series of questions before you give your statements. Akrofi has sworn the Great Oath of the State, supported by our revered fetishes to contradict your charges against him and added that you slandered him. If you can do so, respond to them to make our way clear."

"If you will not listen to any question, permit me to call my ex-husband, as I wish to whisper something into his ears before I make my statement."

A sword-bearer was quickly dispatched and Owusu was brought. Konaduwa then obtained permission to address the court saying:

"My Lords, it is strikingly obvious that many of you think I have given you a lot of trouble. I therefore see that many of you are angry with me. But my lords, permit me to say that when the King of Ashanti had full jurisdiction over this State, and people were mown down like grass before the scythe, no person was killed without being allowed to state his or her defence. Therefore, I pray, do not be prejudiced or biased against me, but, do kindly give me a hearing. I now beg to say that I was sent to the farm by Owusu. The farm is not mine but his. It was he who asked me to go with this man. Had we found any treasure-trove in that farm, it would by custom have been his. In this light, if any case, civil or criminal originated there, it is perspicuously obvious that it is his, and I do not see the reason why he should be free from it. Under the circumstance I swear the Great Oath of the State that Owusu should stand surety for both Akrofi and me in the case."

Some of the people present endorsed her statement, but others, who were prejudiced, remarked that she was too provoking and long-winded. They therefore asked the Omanhene to nullify her oath and arraign her. But the Omanhene was thoughtful. After consulting the Adontenhene, he said he shared views with the woman, therefore he ordered his Linguist to ask Owusu if he had something to say in repudiation to what Konaduwa said.

Owusu stated that when their marriage was dissolved, it lay in his power to administer a fetish oath to the woman by which she would be compelled to confess any conjugal infidelity; but as he liked to nip everything in the bud, he did not do so. Besides, when they returned from the farm that evening, she did not report anything to him; and he had the belief that if no quarrel had arisen, she never would have told him. He therefore did not find his way clear to stand surety for them. He added that he was sure that he was speaking the secret feelings of all the men assembled there.

Okyeame Kwadwo Kuma retorted that according to the customs of the country, when an oath was sworn on some one, he was expected to respond to it before making his statement. But it appeared that Owusu had just made his statement and showed his grounds why he could not stand surety. As that was not their usual routine of settling cases, what he said could not be countenanced. It was therefore incumbent on Owusu to either respond to the oath or to stand surety for them.

Owusu now not knowing what else to do or say, rebutted the oath. Both Konaduwa and Owusu were taken as oath-prisoners, and a fee of eight shillings was collected from each of them. They were then asked to nominate their sureties. Konaduwa called her father and Owusu also called his. When both of these men appeared in court and were informed why they were called there, the two of them then asked for permission to retire for a short consultation before they returned to take the oath of surety.

When they had retired, Owusu's father told Konaduwa's father that, in his opinion, they should not allow their children to argue in open court. He continued that in this country if any woman was conjugally unfaithful, her husband stood surety for her; but if she lost the case, the debt added to her head-money or dowry, pending the final dissolution of the marriage, when the woman paid this and the cost of all such presents as could be claimed. In that case, Owusu had in any case, to stand surety for Konaduwa. But in this particular case, both fathers must jointly stand surety for their children or ask the court to dismiss the case and then share the court fines equally between them. He made it clear to Konaduwa's father that if Akrofi had committed any assault upon Konaduwa, custom demanded that she should have reported it to her husband directly she returned from the farm, even before she took her bath. On her failure to do this, the woman would lose the case if it were tried.

Konaduwa's father clearly understood him. They therefore went back to court, but instead of taking the oath of surety, they asked Opanin Atuobi, the Mankrado of Abetifi, to intercede in the case for both of them. They went to sit by him, and held his feet.

The Mankrado then told the Akyeame that he had been asked to intercede in the case for the two parties, and that therefore the Omanhene should be informed. Okyeame Owusu then asked whether he was interceding in the present case alone or in the original case as well. Opanin Atuobi asked his clients who told him that he should intercede in all the cases. The Adontenhene through Okyeame Owusu asked Konaduwa and Owusu whether they agreed with their fathers in the steps they had taken, or whether they wished to make their arguments in court. They replied that they were not wiser than their fathers, and so could not budge an inch from what their fathers had said. The Omanhene then asked Okyeame Asabere to pronounce judgment against the two men.

Asabere then stood up, lifting up the *Asempa-ye-tia*, that most ancient Linguist's Stick covered with skin of the *adowa*, the smallest brown antelope, who is supposed to be the king of all animals. It had an iron-point end, and the whole stick was clotted with the blood of sheep. Holding it in his left hand and addressing the court amid the great noise made by the court-criers, he began:

"Listen, all you persons here assembled. It is customary that if any person be in need or trouble, his friend or neighbour, who is able, should help him. Akrofi has told us that fettered by poverty and toil, he went to Owusu to obtain a cutlass on credit with which he intended to make a farm. Owusu kindly gave him the tool, and Akrofi fixed his own time for payment. With the cutlass, he made a nice farm in which he grew many kinds of crops. But, the time came and passed without the payment of the cost of the cutlass, so Owusu sent for Akrofi to demand it. Poor Akrofi had no money to honour the bill, so he volunteered to work in his creditor's farm, assuming that the work he did would serve as the interest on the amount he owed. Owusu agreed to this arrangement and asked his wife Konaduwa to take Akrofi to one of his farms. Akrofi, according to his statement, wished to please the woman, so he worked exceedingly hard. Either Konaduwa had compassion on Akrofi, or she had another motive behind the screen of her mind; nobody knows. She told Akrofi to reserve some of his strength for the day he would be working on his own farm; adding that it was ridiculous for him to work until his back breaks or his palms blister for the small sum of eighteenpence. This and some other words which Konaduwa uttered, put a different complexion on the matter; and she, being an astute woman, foresaw that if Akrofi reported the case to her husband, the consequences would not be fair. She therefore adroitly shifted her ground, and began to create these serious criminal charges against Akrofi.

"You will remember that in her statement, she told this court that Akrofi produced the sum of five pounds to hush her, — Akrofi who had been fettered by poverty and toil so that because of a debt of eighteenpence he volunteered to work two days for his creditor. All this goes to prove that the motive behind the screen of the woman's mind was evil. Anyway, Akrofi wishing to prove his innocence, has sworn the Great Oath of this State, supported by our far-searching fetishes *Fofie* and *Obonyame* and *Pra* that he never even contemplated such a crime. Konaduwa on seeing now that either way her cause was hopeless, hardened her heart and sought for other means to keep this court sitting on to let us lose our aim. Here she now stands. Her heart appears to have forgotten any sense of charity, and her obstinacy has become even more deeply rooted. These two gentlemen, how-ever, have by their foresight and forethought endeavoured to nip our intense anger in the bud. They have appealed to the Mankrado of Abetifi to intercede for them. Therefore the Headmen, the

Minor Chiefs, the Wing-Chiefs, the Adontenhene and our most gracious Majesty, the Omanhene, do hereby command me to announce, and it is hereby announced to you that you two now lying prostrate before the Mankrado of Abetifi, on behalf of your children, that if the case had not been brought to this court for the determination of the best judgment, and any of you lifted up any weight, and hit the State with it, and killed or injured it, you would have committed murder. Now, you the representatives of the State who have assembled here, was not this that which you commanded me to say?"

A shout of confirmation arose, and the small drums, the big drums, the talking drums, the horns everything that could make noise sounded, amply supported by the chorus of the court-criers.

Asemma, one of the court-criers, quickly ran to Kwaku Amamfo, the Head-Linguist, and pulling a small bag from his knicker-pocket, poured profusely some white clay with which he freely daubed the right arm of the linguist representing the State as the visible sign of his being without guilt.

The Mankrado appealed to the Benkumhene to reduce the fines and charges for him. The hearing-fee was cut down to *Ntansa*[1] plus *Asiaboom miensa*[2], the neck-tie of the fines. In addition, four sheep were slaughtered.

All these matters having been finished, Asabere then addressed Konaduwa saying:

"Madam, you know that a woman sells tomatoes and garden-eggs, but not flints. You are a very strong woman indeed; but you know that you women are springs which move everything in this world. True, you are not always wrong in the arrangement of your cases; for when a fish goes bad, one cannot say whether the head or the tail decayed first. So now that you are a free woman I advise you to be softer and quieter, so that sooner or later your beautiful teeth and interesting mode of speaking, because

---

[1]   Twenty-four pounds

[2]   Three times 24/- (twenty-four shillings times three)

you stammer; will attract numerous men into your snare out of
whom you will be able to select one to marry, one that will be
a good husband who will look after you and your children."

Konaduwa listened with a supercilious smile, and said:

"Love, like the sparrow, comes and goes; so when a husband's
love is gone, he maltreats the wife, and nothing she does pleases
him any longer. Anyway, I thank you heartily, I am glad that
the whole series of cases have been squashed to-day. I will pass
this night in the deepest sleep."

The Mankrado then summed up the expenses of the case
which amounted to thirty-two pounds, eight sheep and four cases
of gin, each case being four pounds ten shillings. These expenses
were equally divided between the fathers of Owusu and
Konaduwa. Asabere asked both Owusu and Konaduwa to take
the Oath of Union. When Owusu was about to take the Oath,
Akrofi quickly stepped forward and asked Asabere what compensation he was to receive to pacify him. Konaduwa had after
all striven to jail him and to defame his character, and even if
his innocence had been so openly proved, custom required that
he was to have his full share in the court fines as pacification.
The Omanhene ordered that he should be given four pounds and
two bottles of gin. Akrofi bowed in acceptance and in gratitude,
and left the court for his house. Owusu and Konaduwa, each
swore the Oath of Union and declared that there was nothing
outstanding between them.

The Omanhene then asked Konaduwa if her statement
regarding the hundred and fifty pounds in her lost portmanteau
was correct. She knelt down and said it contained a few of her
personal effects, but it was the fear of the case which was then
pending that instigated her to make such charges against the man.
She therefore would not ask for any compensation for she knew
that that young man did not do it intentionally.

The man knelt down and thanked the Omanhene and
Konaduwa. It was ordered that the man should bring two bottles
of gin to seal the case, so that in future, no claim could be made

by either Konaduwa or any of her relatives. The bottles were brought, and one was consumed by the Assembly and the other taken home by Konaduwa.

Before they rose, the Benkumhene obtained permission to speak and said:

"My Lords, all the cases that have detained us in this town for so many days are cases in which this woman is involved. She and her ex-husband Owusu have incurred a debt in the neighbourhood of forty or fifty pounds. I also hear that this same woman has three more other charges pending at this very court. Though she has not asked me to intercede for her, and I do not know whether she will win or lose in those cases, yet by the virtue of my rank as the Benkumhene of this State, I pray that the Omanhene shows his usual mercy to the relatives, especially the father of the woman, and quashes all the three remaining charges."

The Adontenhene then whispered into the ears of the Omanhene, and after a short deliberation between them, the Omanhene proclaimed that they had now sat for quite a long time, therefore the court would be adjourned until two o'clock the next afternoon.

Amenaku then gave his usual cautionary cry of "Sɔreɛ", meaning, "Arise you"! This was addressed to the Omanhene, for he was the first member of the assembly to rise. When he had risen, the other chiefs and their subjects followed. Some praised the Benkumhene for the peaceable suggestion he made, others thought he was too inquisitive and meddlesome to tamper with people's cases in this manner.

CHAPTER 11

Konaduwa's Charges Quashed.
Amoako Marries Her

AT ONE O'CLOCK the next afternoon, the *Botom*, the Omanhene's summoning drum was beaten, and about a quarter of an hour later, it was beaten again, so that at about half past one the court was already full. The chiefs and people of the Left and Right Wings were in position. Later, the minor chiefs followed, and then the Adontenhene came. Not long afterwards, the Omanhene, more gorgeously dressed then ever, and adorned like an idol, made a slow entry.[1] This time he wore a native woven silk cloth[2], and instead of his heavy gold crown, with gold feathers and ferns, he wore a gilded head dress consisting of amulets and some small- sized gourds. The drums were arranged before and behind him. Sword-bearers, stool-carriers, court-criers and every

---

[1] Obeng uses the phrase 'came creeping in', this is not the first time the Omanhene is described in a slightly ridiculous manner. On the whole the author appears to portray the Adontenhene in a more favourable light than the Omanhene. This could be just a bit of local patriotism, but it might have a deeper significance. At the time the narrative of this book takes place, Kwahu was experiencing political upheavals. But added to this, is the ambivalent relationship between Abene, the seat of the Omanhene, and Abetifi, the seat of the Adontenhene. The Adontenhene of Kwahu, according to tradition, is the regent in periods of interregnum. This has the potential of weakening the authority of the Omanhene while giving the Adontenhene power beyond his expected traditional role. Note also that Obeng's wife, Rose Nyante, whom he had abandoned at the time he wrote this book and lived separated from in Abetifi, belonged to the Bretuo clan (as do the Amanhene of Kwahu).

[2] Most probably *kente*.

65

office-holder were in their place of order. The executioners,
dressed in their uniforms, danced and sang their songs of praise.
The drums, gong-gongs, tom-toms and everything creating noise
played their full part.

When His Majesty was seated, he asked the Adontenhene's
Registrar to read aloud the remaining charges against Konaduwa
to enable him to weigh them before he spoke. The Registrar came
forward and opening his charge-book, read:

1. "That you, on the same day, i.e., the fifth day of July, 1913,
   in the town of Abetifi, and in your house, did swear the Great
   Oath of the State and enforced it with fetish oath of *Fofie* and
   Obonyame that your husband must divorce you, contrary to
   the custom of the State. Are you guilty or not guilty?"

   "Guilty, but I can explain."

2. "That you on the same day, and in your premises, did charge
   the Adontenhene's brave warriors who were assembled there
   at that time with cowardice and compared them with *kapok*,
   which is a very comprehensive insult. Are you guilty or not
   guilty?"

   "Not guilty."

3. "That you, on the same day, and in the same town, did say
   that somebody had been bold enough to speak ill against the
   Adontenhene whom we all adore and hold in the highest
   possible reverence; and also against our esteemed Queen-
   Mother as well as the Elders of this town; but you intentionally concealed it, contrary to the custom of the State. Are you
   guilty or not guilty?"

   "Not guilty."

4. "That you, on the day you were arraigned before the Adontenhene for trial, did say openly that the Omanhene would be biased in his judgment, because he is the blood relative of the Adontenhene, and besides, he takes a share of all his fines inflicted in this court. Are you guilty or not guilty?"

Before Konaduwa could reply to the last charge, the Benkumhene rose and begged the Omanhene to forego the charges, and to allow him to intercede on behalf of the woman. He also called the Omanhene's attention to the advice that the proverbial 'Old Woman' gave them the other day; and reminded them that the 'bone of contention' that brought about all these series of cases was nothing but jealousy. But as jealousy, like hunger, afflicts every person, he begged those in authority who had been affected by the brawling and unbridled tongue of the woman to please pardon her.

In fact, when these charges were read, it became clear that Konaduwa was sorely afraid. She sighed deeply, and from a kind of mental depletion, exclaimed that in fact she did not know what induced her to do and say all these. Though the Omanhene smiled, she thought she perceived an iron hand in a velvet glove; and she became pertrified with fear. The Omanhene did not utter a word, for his dignity counselled him to be silent. Besides, sheep had been slaughtered already. Konaduwa could not look anybody in the face. Her gaze faltered and fell.

The Adontenhene asked his Akyeame to throw the intercession of the Benkumhene to the remaining chiefs to sound their minds. As usual, they asked for permission to retire for consultation. There the Benkumhene again said:

"My Lords, it would be superfluous to say that the woman is a very hard-headed and obstinate woman. It is unnecessary to multiply instances of her arrogance; but the reason why I wish to plead for her is that she is but a woman; and as you all know, a woman who has had a fit of jealousy can do anything in the fit of her passion. I think you all heard that she said she did not know what induced her to do and say what she did. She is now becoming conscious of her faults. I therefore appeal to all of you for your whole-hearted support in my intercession."

The Nifahene said. "In so far as this woman has now openly said she did not know what induced her to do and say what she did, I find that she has repented. You all remember in what manner she spoke to me in open court the other day. But, she is a woman, we must not persecute her. If the other chiefs will not desert us, we shall jointly plead for her."

Every other chief promised his full support. This agreement having been completed, they all returned to take their seats. The Nifahene asked the Akyeame to tell the Omanhene that before they informed the court what advice the proverbial 'Old Woman' gave them, he would like to ask Konaduwa one question. He was allowed. Through the Akyeame he asked the woman if she remembered what insulting words she spoke to him in open court the other day. She replied that she did. Having said this she at once asked the *Ohene* of Obomeng to intercede on her behalf.

"I see you are now coming to your senses," the Nifahene said. "I forgive you freely, but be careful of your tongue. It is the softest and smallest part of the body, but it 'breaketh a bone, though itself hath none'. It can either kill or release a man."

"I thank you very much for this piece of advice, my lord," answered Konaduwa.

The Benkumhene's Okyeame then told the Omanhene that the proverbial 'Old Woman' advised them that all the charges against the woman must be quashed, and that she should be very strongly reprimanded. The Omanhene readily pronounced all the charges quashed, but ordered that the many sheep slaughtered during the whole series of cases, should be paid for by the woman. She fell on her knees before his Majesty and thanked him sincerely and confessed that it was nothing but jealousy that pushed her into such infamy. She promised that such conduct would never recur.

Luckily, some of the men whose sheep they had killed came

forward and told her that they would not claim anything for their sheep. Only ten of the many sheep were paid for. Konaduwa was then asked to sign a bond by which she bound herself to be of good behaviour for twelve months, and that in the event of her using bad language to any man, she would have to pay a fine of twenty-five pounds. When the bond was completed and signed, the woman told Asabere that she wanted to say a word. When allowed to speak she said:

"I now find that of late, I have behaved very disgracefully to my former husband, my mother-in-law and my rival[3] in marriage. I therefore beg the Omanhene on my knees to kindly ask the pardon of these people for me."

Everybody was pleased to hear this from a woman who, of late, had been very overbearing in her conduct. All the chiefs supported her plea for forgiveness. They were all pleased to see that after such tremendous storm, profound peace and calm had been restored.

The court rose at about half-past six when lights had been lit. Towards eight o'clock when Konaduwa and her parents were summing up their debt, a tall, dark, slim youth, sparing of speech, walked in, and greeted them politely.

"Who are you?" asked the old man.

"My name if Kofi Amoako," he replied.

"And what do you want here at such an hour of the night?"

Amoako threw diffidence into the air and said: "I came to express my sympathy and congratulations to Madam Konaduwa."

"It is now a late hour to visit a friend, so good night." said the old man.

"But, please, Sir, I would like to see her before I say good night, for she asked me to come and call about this hour."

The father, then beckoned Konaduwa to come. When she came out, she shook hands with him in the exchange of greetings,

---

[3] Text B has changed this word to *my husband's other wife ,* but 'rival' is what most Ghanaians would use to refer to a co-wife.

and she gave him a seat. Amoako broke the silence that followed by saying: "I came to express to you my sympathy and congratulations because of the happy ending of your case. I hear all the charges have been quashed, and you are now a free woman."

She replied that what he had heard was correct, but they still needed to raise a loan to pay back what they had borrowed. Amoako told her that if they failed to obtain any loan here, he would go to Abuakwa to raise the money there. He therefore asked her the exact amount they needed. The old man, who overhead their conversation, interrupted by saying that the total cost of the case was close to fifty pounds; but this was to be shared between him and Owusu's father, so their actual share was therefore twenty-five pounds.

Amoako promised to write to his father at Anyinam, who, he felt sure, could let them have this amount, and without any interest. He then bade them good-night, and departed.

In less than five days, he returned to tell the old man that his father was ready to put up the money, on condition that Konaduwa would marry his son Amoako. Amoako's father had seen her when she was on her way going to Asiakwa, and there he had expressed the desire that because of her pearly teeth and of her stammering, he would like to have her in his family.

Konaduwa's mind was sounded by her mother, who said that because of her hard-headedness, she would not allow her to go to marry at Akyem.[4] But Konaduwa said that experience had made her more careful and much wiser, so she could marry from any part of the country peacefully. Her maternal relatives were then informed of the suitor.

That very day another young man from one of the neighbouring villages came to ask for Konaduwa's hand. Her relatives wished her to marry him, but she did not agree. Many more suitors came in every other day, but she rejected them all.

------

[4]   There is the perception among the Kwahus, that the Akims are quarrelsome and litigious.

It was pointed out to her that it was better and much safer for a person to marry from her home town, but she asked. "If that were true, why did Owusu divorce me?" Every day more and more suitors arrived; but she was resolute.

One day her father called her aside and told her that the suitors were daily increasing. Some were men of high rank politically, some commercially and others educationally. She had therefore to make her choice, else she would in the end lose all. She told her father that a house may hold a hundred men, but the heart of a woman has only room for one of them. She had made her choice already. Of all the myriads of suitors, Amoako had won her heart. That evening, Amoako visited the house, and she told him what conversation had taken place between her and her father. Elated by this, Amoako hastily asked his landlord to go and ask Konaduwa's father to give her to him in marriage.

Amoako brought the 'knocking fees,' which were instantly followed by the preliminary presents to the woman and her relatives. These were immensely pleased with the presents, and so Amoako was presented with his intended wife. The woman who went to ask and those who presented her got their due fees.

Four days later Amoako was asked to place the head-rum. Four bottles of whisky and eight of soda were brought. The father took half and sent the other half to Konaduwa's relatives. Before they drank the spirits, one of the men assembled there said it was necessary that the marriage laws of the State be put before Amoako, as he was a stranger. A linguist was therefore called in for that purpose, and he reminded them that certain fees in connection with the marriage were to be paid into the coffers of the Adontenhene. This was to be done because in his marriage registration book, the date of the marriage, the names of the couple, the rank of the man, and his adultery fees were to be recorded for future reference.

The Okyeame then repeated to Amoako's landlord, for the information of Amoako the following bye-laws:

1. If Amoako marries another woman or has a concubine, and through jealousy the wife commits suicide, he is not held responsible. He would only have to procure the ordinary materials for the funeral of a wife, viz, a coffin, a pillow, cloths, waist beads, a fathom of silk, a mat and a sheep and a quantity of drinkables, and gun power for firing at the funeral. So also if the woman becomes conjugally unfaithful, and through jealousy the man commits suicide, the woman is not held responsible. She is to procure the necessary materials for the funeral.

2. If the man fails to feed the woman, and she steals any food or anything like that, the man is to be held responsible for the theft.

3. If the woman accompanies her husband to his country, and through a quarrel or other, she incurs any debt, the husband must pay.

4. If she is in her own country and through a quarrel or anything she incurs any debts, the relatives have to pay.

5. When the woman is attacked by any ordinary sickness, the expenses must be born by her husband.

6. If through adultery she contracts any venereal disease, the husband does not care for her medical attendance.[5]

7. If she borrows any beads or trinkets for her personal adornment from the relatives of her husband, when she is in the town of the husband, and these get lost, the husband is to make any compensation which will be claimed by his relatives. On the other hand, if it is found out that she has kept

---

[5]   Text B has omitted this clause

those things, and told a lie that they had been lost or stolen, it is turned into stealing. In this case, the man will share the expense with her relatives. Because if those articles were not found, they would become her family property.

8. If any other man carry on an intrigue with her, she has to confess at once to enable her husband to collect his dues there and then. If she fails to report it at once, and the offender leaves the State or dies, she has to pay the adultery fees.

9. If the woman finds any treasure-trove or discovers any valuable thing in the street or anywhere, she should give it untouched to her husband, who in turvn will bring it untouched to the relatives of the woman before they give him his share. If he keeps it, or tampers with it, at the dissolution of the marriage, any expense he has made on the woman, including her head-money, will be forfeited.

10. The man has full right to claim presents, in the form of cash, cloths, and kerchiefs, made to the woman dring their marriage. If the cloths are torn, the rags should be produced in evidence. If they were stolen or lost, and the husband knew of this fact, they cannot be claimed.

11. The children produced form the marriage belong to the woman, but they are to. be brought up by the father, and some of them sent to school. They are to be fully trained for their future living. But if he should be in debt, and need money, he has no right to ask any of them to stand surety for a loan anywhere, except he has obtained the full consent of the woman's relatives.

12. If the woman travels with her husband, and stays away for a long time, and he gives any marriage presents to her when

they are still away, the husband cannot claim those presents. If the man thinks those articles are too valuable to be presented free, he should keep them until they come home, then they should be presented before her relatives. In this case, the man has to tell truly the correct cost of those articles.

13. If because of the exceptionally good services of the woman the husband wishes to forego the claim of presents in clause 12 above, the said husband must support his intention with the Great Oath of the State; then the relatives of the woman have to bring some bottles of gin, the quantity is according to the value of the articles presented, to seal the presention and validity of the presentation.

14. At the dissolution of the marriage, the man has full right to ensure the conjugal fidelity of the woman by the administering of a fetish oath. In case of an ordinary man, viz, a man who does not hold any stool in the town or State, this oath is administered on three points. In the case of a Stool Elder, upon many points, according to the customs of the various States.

Amoako wanted to ask for the amendment or modification of some of the above clauses, but this was refused; and since he did not like to lose the woman, he yielded to all the clauses.

After a few days' stay, Amoako asked the permission of his new relatives-in-law to take his wife to his country to show her to his father and the other relations. Permission was granted, but he was told that owing to the wide difference between the marriage customs of the two countries, he should remove from his state to settle permanently in the state of his wife. He promised to consult his parents without whose sanction he could not definitely agree to their request.

When Amoako arrived home, he explained to his father and his maternal uncles all what he had been told, and asserted that because of the genuine love he had for his wife, he was quite willing to move from his country to stay with his wife. They were sorry that he should feel like that, but as they all knew that love is blind and deaf, they could not thwart him. They all readily approved of his proposal; and allowed him to migrate to stay in his wife's country.

They were married for several years, and had many children. Owing to her previous experience, Konaduwa became the best wife and a very good mother and house-keeper; and as the fairy-tale puts it, they lived happily ever after.

CHAPTER 12

The Trial of Abire

IT IS a fixed custom among the Akans that the word "Fool" is not spoken to any man by a woman. This offence is punishable with the slaughter of sheep and a fine. Unfortunately, through excessive anger Abire recklessly pronounced this word to Kwabena Somua, the Chief Sword-Bearer. This was made worse by the rude and insulting question which she put to him, saying; "Have you got your eyes at your anus?"[1] This too was an outrageous utterance. This made matters even worse for Abire. Two sheep were therefore slaughtered. As explained earlier, Abire had been sent by a friend Afriyie; a fore-leg of each sheep was therefore sent to Abire, who in turn sent them to Afriyie. The court did not know this, so when the hearing day was fixed, the hearing notice was sent to Abire. The day came.

About seven o'clock in the morning, the summoning drum of the Adontenhene was beaten for the first time, to announce to the people that a case would be heard that day. Half an hour later, the second notice was given. The courtiers and the elders began to take their positions, and shortly afterward, the Adontenhene arrived. He was very simply dressed as usual. He wore a native woven silk cloth with a pink silk eucorah around his waist. He wore ordinary leathern sandals. His head-gear was of pink silk with an amulet covered with lion skin on the foreheard; the knot was artistically tied, the ends stood up, showing on each side of the head. On the breast he wore three or four amulets covered with the skin of a leopard; and at each elbow

---

[1]   Text B has replaced this rather profane outburst with "Have you no eyes in your head?"

he wore many gourds covered with silver and gold. On each finger of the right hand he wore many proverbial gold rings, consisting of a tortoise, a snail, a fish and a bird picking something on her back; and on the thumb he had one crab. The left hand was free of rings; but in the palm he held a beautiful silk hand-kerchief which he used to wipe off the mouth when he felt that the edges were moist. In his mouth there was a pipe, the tube being a hollowed reed, five feet long, spangled here and there at measured intervals of one foot with silver plates. This was fixed in a bowl of clay baked and ebonised with the sap of a vine. At the tip a narrow mouth-piece of silver had been fixed. The bowl was made in the form of a man carrying a keg of a gun-power. At the middle of the keg which the man was carrying on his head, there was a hole into which good scented tobacco had been put. A servant sitting at the farther end was fanning the fire burning the tobacco by blowing into it. The Adontenhene's stool was placed on a piece of elephant hide measuring about eight feet square; his feet rested on a footstool.

As usual when he walked through the crowd to his seat, everybody stood up, and kept standing when the servant cried and yelled to show everybody that the owner of the land had arrived there. The people remained standing until he was seated. The court-criers shouted "Audience!" Drums were beaten, horns were blown; and after this din of noise, silence fell. The Adontenhene then asked Okyeame Safo to inquire from the Registrar the number of cases they had on the list. He replied that there were only four, the first of which was Abire's case. She was then asked to stand up to listen to her charges. They were read as follows:

1. That you, on the eighth day of July, 1913, in the town of Abetifi, did use an insulting word, which custom forbids shall be used to an ordinary man, to Kwabena Somua, the Chief Sword-Bearer of the Adontenhene, to wit; "foolishly" contrary to the custom of the State. What is your plea, guilty or not guilty?"

She pleaded guilty with explanation.

2.   That you, on the same date and at the same spot did ask
     Kwabena Somua, the Chief Sword-Bearer of the Adontenhene,
     whether he had got his eyes at his anus; contrary to the
     custom of the State. What is your plea, guilty or not guilty?"

She pleaded guilty with explanation.

She was then asked to nominate her surety in the case, who
should promise on an oath to pay all expenses of the case should
she be found guilty. She nominated Afriyie, who was accordingly
sent for. They told her what Abire said, and after a short deliberation, she declined to stand surety. She explained that she
only asked Abire to carry her bridal food to her husband. Abire
knew Kwabena Somua full well, as well as the high post he
held. If therefore he unintentionally knocked her down, she
ought to have held her tongue, and not abused him.
     This explanation was not accepted in its entirety on the
grounds that had Abire picked a nugget or any other valuable
thing in the street when she was on her errand, Afriyie would
rightly claim a share. Afriyie replied that in that case, she could
claim only a share, but not the whole treasure, therefore she could
not understand why she alone was asked to stand surety for
Abire.
     In this light, Abire was asked to nominate another person
in addition to Afriyie. She sent for her father who readily came.
     As stated above, the court was quite full to its utmost
capacity, for everybody was eager to hear how this sensational
case would be tried. Afriyie's father and Abire's jointly swore
the oath of surety, and she was sent into the witness-box. She
gave her statement as follows:
     "My name is Adoma-Hemmaa, but because of my dark
complexion, I am called Abire. I live in this town, and I am a
farmer by profession. Not very long ago, I was in the street

talking with a friend of mine, when Afriyie beckoned me. When I went, she told me that she had just finished cooking her husband's food; but as she did not want to carry it herself, she requested me to send it for her. I ran quickly home to tell my mother that I was being sent by my friend Afriyie. My mother advised me to carry the food carefully and be sure not to fall. On my way, I heard the beating of drums, the blowing of horns and much noise from the palace. I did not know what had happened, but when I found that the streets were thronged with people, it struck me that something unusual had happened. As women naturally take no part in such cases, I did not pay any attention, but just continued with my load. Suddenly I heard someone running. When turning my head in that direction to see what was the matter, this man, pointing to Kwabena Somua, the Chief Sword-Bearer, in his eagerness to rush into the palace, knocked me over, and upset the tray of food. I was especially upset because the other wife of my friend's husband happened to be there. She saw the accident, she saw the dishes shattered to pieces, yet she ran quickly to her house, and when she returned she had dressed in white satin and blanched herself with powder. She was exultant, saying how exeedingly glad she was that that food did not reach their husband, for Afriyie was a much better cook than herself. She danced about hopping here and there like a bird in a cage. All her movements spelled vengeance. When I remembered the money my friend spent in preparing the dishes and how such a good food had been wasted, and how her husband and his friends would be so sorely disappointed when the food did not arrive, I lost all self-control; and in my rage, I spoke those words. At that time, though I knew Kwabena Somua's rank for he was holding his sword, I forgot all about him and of the sorrowful consequences, so that like a little child, I babbled those words which I now dare not repeat. That was why I pleaded guilty and asked permission to explain that I uttered those words inadvertently, and so upon my knees I most humbly ask the pardon of the court and of Kwabene Somua, hoping my offence will be forgiven. I penitently retract all what I said. Here am I, I lie prostrate under the respectable man whom I have so offended, and submissively beseech his pardon."

On saying this, she was asked to stand up. She wiped off the tears streaking her cheeks. Her father and the other surety bent their knees, and implored the court to forgive the offence and to minimise the punishment.

The Adontenhene was much touched with the remorseful address of the attrite woman, and said: "How true it is that women are of different kinds. What a vast difference there is between Konaduwa and this woman!"

He then asked the jury to retire for consultation. When they were there deliberating over the verdict, the leader said: "Gentlemen of the jury, let us consider the case sympathetically, Abire has pronounced herself "guilty", but let us remember her feelings and modify the verdict. If you all will agree with me, I would suggest that she is treated leniently. The Adontenhene is rather to be advised to step upon it with his broad sandals. The woman is almost innocent. She did not say those words with intention or with any sobriety; but as some sheep have been slaughtered already, she and the woman who sent her should bear the cost. Apart from this, no other punishment is to be inflicted upon the woman. Is there any one amongst you who do not feel sympathy for this woman? If so, let him speak. If any of you were in the place of the woman, surely you would have acted with much more vehemence and would have probably come to blows. I wait for your individual opinions, gentlemen."

"I agree with you," said one of the gentlemen of the jury.

"So do I," said another.

"And I concur." "And I support" chorused the rest.

They therefore returned to the court to deliver their verdict. They stated that Abire did not intentionally utter those forbidden words to the chief of the sword-bearers; for her feelings were either hurt or perturbed by the sudden accident; and in consideration of the food that was lost, which from a woman's point

of view was naturally distressing, they could by no means pronounce her guilty. They therefore begged the Adontenhene to
kindly 'step upon the case.'

The court readily agreed to the decision of the jury, and Abire
was asked to pay the cost of the two sheep that were slaughtered,
and go scot free.

When Afriyie's husband, who was at the court and greatly
disturbed, heard of the verdict, he rose to his feet, and followed
by many of his friends, he went round the assembly, thanking
the Ohene, the Elders and the jury. There in front of everybody,
he opened his portmanteau, and pulled out a number of currency
notes covering the cost of the sheep. Before he paid the fine
he said:

"My Lords, permit me to advise my wife and all the other
women who have assembled here now. There is nothing which
is more pleasant to a man than to see his wife serving him. If
my wife had not been shy of bringing the food herself, this
accident and all that came in its wake could have been averted,
and it would have pleased me all the more. If a wife is diligent
in the care of her husband, especially when there is a rival, she
strengthens the bond of love that binds them together. This
softens the heart and feelings of the man and inclines him towards
such an attentive woman, so that he becomes very grateful to
her always because of her indefatigable services. This being the
case, he does not count the cost when he makes any presents
to such a woman. I intended to make my wife an expensive
gift of silk cloth and some head-kerchiefs which I wished to give
her in the presence of my friends who were with me at the time,
when she should have carried that food herself to my house; but
alas, that was not the case! I therefore candidly advise the
women here assembled that they must never be ashamed
when they are performing domestic duties for their husbands."

He then paid the amount to the Okyeame, and bending
down, he pulled out the silk cloth which was woven locally and
the silk head-kerchiefs and gave them to his wife, else some

people might say his words were just an empty boast. He then put his arm around his wife, and went away with her from the assembly.

The Head of the court-criers then shouted, and the Head of the palanquin carriers seconded it with a much louder noise to notify the people that the Adontenhene was about to rise. The former shouted at the top of his voice saying: "*Sɔre ɛɛɛ!*" The potentate then stood up, adjusted his cloth and began to move. According to custom, they left the court in the same order by which they came. The drums, horns, people, everybody talked and the noise that was there was unimaginable. The Krontihene moved at a snail's pace, and hindered the progress of the Adontenhene, so a sword-bearer was asked to go and tell him to 'move-on'; but he refused, saying that his royalty did not permit him to move any faster. He continued in such a doubly slow march until the Adontenhene pacified him with a beautiful cloth of native weave. Having received this, he quickened his pace considerably, but not very long afterwards, he came to a halt, looking here and there, and unwilling to move. Another messenger went to urge him to move on, but he was obdurate. A handsome present of eight pounds was sent to him again with an humble request that it was getting to sunset, and besides, rain was threatening, and unless he hurried, the whole show would be spoilt. He then went in a good pace, and the gathering was thus able to disperse before the downpour began.

CHAPTER 13

The Abundant Harvest.
Akrofi Weds

TO RETURN to Akrofi. When he was declared innocent of the heavy charges laid· upon him by Konaduwa, he went back to his agricultural labour. From the small farm he tilled at first, he raised an astounding harvest which made him love farming all the more. The onions, tiger-nuts, monkey-nuts and corn which he harvested were easily sold to his customers who came from every part of the Colony with their sacks. At the end, when he counted his proceeds, he was highly delighted to find himself comparatively well off.

He therefore engaged two Hausa labourers at a reasonable wage, who helped him to enlarge his farms. Several acres were tilled, the ground dug and beds were raised. People who passed by and saw the trouble he took in digging so deeply and raising beds in European style, were greatly surprised and amused, for to their minds he was wasting time and strength and money. They pointed out to him that from time immemorial their ancestors had been doing the farms in the old way, yet had reaped appreciable harvests, therefore it was sheer folly on the part of Akrofi to go to so much trouble. But as hard as they tried, they could not understand why Akrofi wasted such time and money so unnecessarily.

Akrofi, to satisfy them, explained that he had stayed with a European miner at Oboase where he was employed as a gardener. There he learned that to farm by "the rule of thumb" was not only ridiculous, but entirely useless in the right sense of the word. But, they could not understand this, nor see why he laid out such a large farm, and planted short hedges between the various sections. They thought this was not at all necessary; for to farm by the "rule of thumb" all the different kinds of crops are planted or sown at random all over the farm. Yams, corn, onions, pepper, cassava, ground- and tiger-nuts, and what not, were grown together in confusion. What puzzled them the more was the distances between the crops which he patiently measured.

He slowly but surely carried out the work until the whole farm was staked out and planted. By this time all the other farmers had sown their crops which were germinating. He then raised his beds and sowed. He knew when the rains were to be expected; and made full use of the knowledge. Soon the farm was entirely covered with a mantle of green, and the crops were very healthy. He carefully kept the farm free from weeds, and repatedly told his labourers the harm these could do to the cultivated crops.

Once, while on one of his daily rounds, he found some insects which he furiously attacked and killed. A friend of his who was there thought Akrofi was getting mad. He rushed there eagerly and inquired whether he had seen a snake. Akrofi told him that he was killing some insects, because they would spoil his farm. With not a little astonishment, that friend laughed at him and said it is a bad workman who quarrels with his tools. Akrofi then told the man that he learned from his European master that weeds are very injurious to plants, for they form a hiding-place for insects; they rob the plants of their food and prevent them from receiving sufficient air. Quietly, that man left Akrofi with the mind that he was going mad.

He asked his labourers to gather the weeds which they had weeded and put them in a heap so that in the course of time they would become good humus for manuring the farm and for lining the holes when permanent trees would be planted. The farm was kept very tidy and as it was not far from the town, many people walked there to see it for amusement. The yams were staked with long and thick poles, and vines pruned. That farm was really a sight worth seeing, and it was regarded as a "model farm" in the vicinity.

As a result of his labour, the first crops of yams proved so fine that everybody was astonished. They were easily sold out. The holes underneath the harvested yams were deepened and enlarged to allowed the second crops to grow bigger still. The corn and the other half-year crops, such as onions, and ground-nuts were also very abundant and quickly sold. Money was coming in, gradually at first, then faster. Akrofi was highly delighted. With the money he thus obtained, he engaged more labourers whom he ordered to make a cocoa farm for him.

Because Akrofi dug his farm so carefully and did all the work in it in the European style, no other farmer or gardener matched him in the richness of his harvest. People began to think that he had some supernatural power with which he worked, because he reaped everything in much more abundance than any other farmer whose farm was about three or four times larger than Akrofi's. Any explanation he gave them was rejected; but he thought the people were simple-minded and that was why they could not understand; for it was a waste of time trying to make them see why such a small farm could yield such abun-dance.

Wishing to obtain suitable land for a cocoa farm, he ap-proached the Omanhene for a site. He was instructed to go into the forest to see if he could find any site which was suitable to him, so off he went. He roamed here and there in the primeval forest; but everywhere he went he found that large farms of cocoa had already been made. According to the customs of the State, he could not begin a farm anywhere near existing ones unless he had obtained the sanction of their owners. This being the case, hard as he tried, he could not find a suitable site.

He went farther into the land and crossed a stream beyond which he found no farms. He carefully scoured the length and breadth of the land, but all what he found was that four rivers flowed through it. The soil was deep for he thrust a sharpened stick into it which went down for nearly one yard. He also found that the soil was porous for he could easily pull out some young plants with little or no effort.

Being satisfied with his prize, he cut several pieces of stick about one yard long, split one end of each in two and wedged a folded leaf in each, and fixed them several feet apart. This was done to show anyone who should happen to come there, that this particular land had been earmarked by somebody for farming. Having done this, he left the labourers there after they had been instructed to make some huts and thatch them for their temporary abode. He then returned to the capital to report his success to the Omanhene. He went with the usual drinks.

Later the Omanhene sent some of his servants to go with Akrofi and see if the land about which he told him had not been cultivated or already earmarked by somebody else for cultivation. This entailed more expenses, because the Omanhene's servants would not move a step without something being paid to them. Refreshments, provisions and several other things were procured by purchase, and arrangements were made for their transport. On their arrival, they were highly pleased to see that huts had already been made and temporary bedsteads fixed in them. One of the labourers had killed some game with his master's double- barrelled gun, and so a hearty meal was placed before them. Before they went to bed, they drained not a few bottles of liquor.

Early next morning, after their bath, they drank some more to whet their appetite, and then breakfasted before they went to inspect the land. They found that all what Akrofi had told the Omanhene was correct. There was no farm nearby. They therefore, in the name of the Omanhene, permitted him to make any farm he liked, and told him that in future, should anybody send in any application for a site for farming, he could assign a portion to him. Akrofi made them several presents again before they were accompanied back home.

Akrofi went round the land again and selected a site between two streams where he thought the land was well watered.

Several acres were cultivated. The trees were felled, the branches and the twigs were cut into small pieces. In due course the field was dry and fire was applied to it, and the leaves were burnt to ashes. The debris was collected in heaps and burnt again, and the farm was ready for planting. He did not wait too long for rain. Akrofi remembered, that when on his food farm he allowed a good distance between the crops, he reaped the richest harvest amongst all the farmers. He therefore decided to do the same on his new farm, when he planted the cocoa seedlings. But he was at a loss to know the correct distances to allow, for the white man from whom he gleaned his knowledge about farming was not a cocoa grower. He therefore left the labourers there and went home. After a few days stay for preparation, he proceeded down to Aburi to consult an Agricultural Officer who was in charge of the Botanical Gardens there.

Before he set out, he was persuaded by nearly all his friend not to go. They asked him why he was so much bent upon spending his money so unnecessarily. In those days there were no good roads, and consequently no bicycle, or lorry or train was available. It then took a very good walker five clear days to make the journey from Abetifi to Aburi. The section from Mpraeso to Anyinam was the worst. Mud was waist deep at several places, and many thorny brambles and tree stumps lay hidden in it. Big trees uprooted by strong gales lay here and there across the paths, so that sometimes one had to walk for about half a mile in the bush to circumvent that barrier. In many cases one might unexpectedly knock one's head against a hive of wasps or another species of these insects and be mercilessly stung. There were no villages at which to halt, so before one embarked on such a journey, one had to take a good supply of already cooked food along. This meant that the traveller had to rise early in the morning to boil a few coco-yams or plantains which he mashed with pepper and onion and salt and wrapped in a plantain leaf which had been passed over a flame to make it flexible. This would be the only food of the traveller for the whole day. You can therefore well imagine how tedious and troublesome travelling was in those days.

In spite of all these impediments, Akrofi was determined to obtain the advice of an Agricultural Officer before he planted his cocoa. He prepared fully, and left one morning unseen by any of his friends.

He toiled and trudged along this dangerous path until he reached Anyinam in the evening of the third day. Knowing that he had made the worst part of the whole journey, he rested there for two nights. When he reached Aburi and saw the Curator, as that Officer was officially named, he was very happy. The Curator too was equally pleased to see that in order to seek horticultural advice, Akrofi had travelled such a distance by such a dangerous path. The next morning, Akrofi gave the officer some presents of eggs and fowls and groundnuts, which he accepted with the remark: "It's very good of you to bring me these." He then told Akrofi to put in his cocoa seedlings at fifteen feet apart on level land and at ten feet apart on a slope. He also advised him to plant plantains and coco-yams and bananas between them to protect the young trees from the torrid heat of the sun; and added that at about forty-five feet apart he should plant permanent shade trees such as funtumia or kola trees, to receive dew and preserve moisture when the trees matured. This was not all. The Curator gave Akrofi a good quantity of coffee, both Arabica and Liberica varieties; some kinds of pear seedlings in a box; suckers of dwarf and copper bananas; some thorny -and queen-apples, and also some imported pawpaw seeds. Akrofi asked the kind Curator how much he had to pay for all these things, and was dumbfounded to hear that they were given gratis. Seedlings of sweet orange and tangerine were also added.

Luckily Akrofi had brought with him four of his labourers, and having found some more carriers from the neighbourhood, he prepared to return home, after he had profoundly thanked the Curator for his generosity.

Seeing how grateful he was, the Curator asked him if he would like some seedlings of white kola and coconuts. Akrofi replied that he could not afford the transport. But the kind Curator managed it. He was in need of some lion, leopard and monkey skins and some crocodile eggs. All these were very common in Kwahu, so Akrofi told the man that he could easily obtain some for him and send them by a carrier. After a moment's thought, the Curator assembled all the workmen in the Gardens and selected four of them to accompany Akrofi to bring back those products which were very urgently wanted for the wife of His Excellency the Governor who would soon visit Aburi on account of her health.

Akrofi's heart jumped up into his mouth because of joy. He then said "Good-bye" to the white man and departed with his men. They slowly trotted on and on until they safely arrived at Abetifi. After three days' stay for rest there, Akrofi obtained from the Adontenhene two lion skins and two beautiful leopard skins. From another hunter he obtained eight monkey skins and six crocodile eggs. These being ready and well packed so that the eggs would not break, he sent the carriers back to Aburi with a letter informing the Curator that they were all presented to him in token of gratitude for all his kindness.

Akrofi then found some more carriers and with his prize he went back into his farm. He dug holes at measured distances which he lined with humus and then planted all the plants he brought from Aburi. Nobody understood what he was doing. They laughed and derided him as usual; but he was resolute like a rock. He then planted bananas and plantains and coco-yams and permanent shade trees at reasonable intervals as he had been instructed to at Aburi. At other plots he put in pears, oranges and other fruits. On another plot he put in a large quantity of yams, and on another onions, and on another nuts and corn. He paid greater attention to the half-yearly crops, as these paid much quicker than the annual, and this enabled him to engage many more labourers.

Now that he was prospering and his wealth had increased, Akrofi made up his mind to find a wife, but a thrifty and industrious one. As you are aware, he was never in a hurry. He thought over this question for a long time, and unlike other young men, he did not rush. He cast glances in different houses to see where he could find a wife who would be his help-mate, but not one who would be a millstone around his neck and sink him in the depths of the ocean.

There was a gentleman nearby who had three beautiful daughters, so he contrived to visit that house occasionally; hiding his intention, until he had watched each girl's behaviour and assessed her mode of speech.

One day when he went there, the three girls were sitting round a table, their parents were in another room. He first greeted the parents and then the girls. Their father being slightly astonished to see him there, inquired if he brought any message for them. Akrofi politely replied that he was returning from a friend's house, and seeing that they were at home, he came there to greet them and to inquire after their health. They were highly pleased to hear this, and thanked him. They then asked him to stay for a chat. He thanked them courteously and accepted a chair.

When he was there, he overheard the eldest girl asking one of her sisters to leave her work and go to the kitchen to prepare food for lunch. This girl refused to go and asked the elder why she could not go and do the cooking herself. For this refusal she was reproached by the youngest girl who said that the eldest girl represented their mother, so she was perfectly right to ask any of them to do any work she liked. A quarrel then ensued, and as the noise was growing, their mother called them and asked them to explain what the argument was about.

Akrofi sat still and watched each of them and heard how they spoke to their mother. His keen gaze attracted the attention of their father who thought that the keenness with which the visitor listened to and watched the girls surely purported something. The mother gave her judgment after all of them had spoken; and remarked that when a visitor was in the house, they ought to have kept quiet. The two elderly girls looked at Akrofi and remarked that he was not a visitor of consequence — only a farmer. The youngest girl told them that the food about which they quarrelled was obtained from a farmer, and pointed out to them that they could not possibly live for one day without the farmers. Akrofi smiled and thanked the girl for defending his profession. He then took his leave and departed.

The two older girls were remarkably beautiful, and the youngest was quite plain. He did not like the tone of the attractive ones and he did not like to select a plain woman as wife. That night he had insomnia. He heard the clock chime all the hours and half-hours till the following morning. He had no friend whom he could consult, and the next day found him still thinking deeply.

One day he sat under a shade tree in the street where many other men, young and old, were sitting, chatting. They conversed about divers matters, and some of them happened to speak about marriage. A plain woman happened to pass by, whose husband had divorced all his other wives, though they were infinitely more beautiful than this one. The men wondered why, though she was the ugliest of all her rivals, her husband retained her. They tossed this problem here and there, until a man, more advanced in age, solved it for them. He told them that it is love, not beauty that governs the world; and that love and joy are inseparable.

"When a man is seeking a wife," the man continued, "the first thing he has to do is to see if he has a spark of love for the woman he is about to select. He cannot possibly love one with whom he is not likely to live happily. Many young men rush into marriage without making any test of their feelings. They do not think whether the 'loved one' can mend a shirt or cook a pudding; but they simply fall in love as the phrase goes. But soon afterwards they find that the clever hands of a woman are far more valuable than her bright glances and cherry cheeks.

And if the shirt and pudding qualifications be absent, then woe to the unhappy man and woe to the unhappy woman. They embark on their life-journey quickly and thoughtlessly like a vessel that is sent to sea without a rudder; and soon they become stranded on the shore of life. They then try as hard as they can to untie that knot which God, the Church and the Law have tied. Many have thus undergone pitiful shipwreck, and yet many more are trying and striving for beauty, thinking that would make them happy. But surely beauty is like a bubble upon the water — no sooner caught than burst. It is likened unto boot polish which brightens the leather for but a few minutes; walk over half a mile and the lustre is gone. It is also like a beautiful and sweet scented flower. In the morning it is admirable; but towards the evening it withers. This being the case, you young men, if you are about to select a wife, you must first see whether the woman whom you are about to choose has sufficient training to fit her for her duties in real life. A woman's education should be conducted throughout with a view to her future position as wife, mother and a house-wife. If you overlook these qualities, and you allow yourself to be caught by the glance of her bright eye, a pair of cherry cheeks and by a handsome figure, then woe unto you. I say this because the enjoyment which you thought you would have soon turns into bitterness, and life becomes like a journey taken barefooted amongst prickles and thorns and briers."

Akrofi pondered over the old man's speech and sighed deeply. The other young men talked and laughed. Some remarked that once "beauty" is present, nothing else would attract their attention. That night Akrofi continued meditating over the speech and decided that he would no more concern himself with beauty, but with the hands that could mend a shirt and cook a pudding.

He then visited another family who had but two daughters. Both of them were equally beautiful like Aphrodite; but the elder, in truth was a goddess. Akrofi was at once captivated by their beauty and politeness; and so he was in a dilemma to select one. With his usual tact and patience, he decided to frequent that house so as to hear their speech and see how they behaved. Any time he went there, he saw both of them working together. Some other times he met both of them weeding in their mother's vegetable garden. Both liked singing alike, and their voices were like the nightingale's. For more than three months he paid them constant, but irregular visits, but all times he met both of them equally busy. During the whole period, he only greeted them and passed on to converse with their parents.

One day when their parents were in the house, he went to the girls in the vegetable garden to converse with them. Both of them passed their test with distinction. Akrofi was still left in suspense. Luckily, he chanced to find the "Open Sesame" which solved the problem for him.

This girls were picking vegetables and putting them into a basket. As the youngest girl hurried to bring them indoors, some of the pepper dropped. When she was returning to pick them up, she struck her big toe against a tree-stump and cut herself so painfully that she could not help crying. The elder sister began to abuse her and said she was a fool to bother so much about a mere wound. The younger girl, with tears streaking on both cheeks, said: "Little drops of water make the mighty ocean". Saying this, she dried her face and smiled.

As you can imagine, Akrofi was well pleased with the short and pithy answer. He was a farmer and wanted a wife who was both thrifty and industrious. These qualities combined in the younger girl. He therefore, without the least hesitation asked for her hand and after a short preparation, they were married. His choice left him nothing to regret, for the behaviour and house-keeping of the woman left nothing to be desired.

CHAPTER 14

Further Prosperity

AKROFI TOOK his wife to his village. The day before their departure, they went round their relatives and said good-bye to them. That evening their friends visited them for a farewell party.

Early in the morning, their luggage carriers rose and were astir. The bride was eager to go and see her husband's farm of which many people had spoken. The path was not good, therefore they could not travel in any conveyance. As his bride was accustomed to a beautiful house, Akrofi feared she would not be happy in her new surroundings, but luckily, that was not the case. As soon as they crossed the stream, and she saw the farms containing plantain and coco-yarms, she began to be happy. She admired the size of the leaves of the coco-yams, and said, she had never seen any of their size before. In less than three-quarters of an hour, they arrived at their village home.

The labourers had put everything in order, and the whole place was spotlessly clean. Shortly after their arrival, the bride changed and went to the kitchen herself to see what the labourers were doing, and found them playing a new game which she had not seen before. While they were thus engaged, she began to cut yams to prepare her husband's food. The servants assisted and they all partook of the meal.

In the afternoon, she asked her husband to take her over the farm. First they visited the vegetable plot and she was highly pleased with the tidiness of the place and with the size of the crops. From there they went into the fruit plot, where she was pleased to see the oranges, mangoes, pears and others. Besides, she was highly pleased to see them planted in rows and at equal distances. Her husband explained to her that he did so to allow air and sufficient plant food to the trees. Next they looked at the palms and then the kola and funtumia plots. From there they went to the cocoa farm which was the largest of the plots, and thence to the coffee plots, where a hedge of lantana separated the Arabica and Liberica varieties. The labourers had cleared these areas and so it was a pleasure to walk around them.

They returned home at sunset to find their food had been set on the table. After the evening bath they dined and then played a gramophone which one of Akrofi's friends had given him as a wedding present.

The labourers had never seen nor heard one before, so when it began to play, some ran away from the house, but the bolder ones were curious and came nearer to see what was the matter. The first record was a conversation between two Europeans which was interspersed with laughter. They were quite amazed to hear that a machine could talk, and sing and laugh. Those who ran away were persuaded to come back, and all the labourers gathered around to listen to it.

In the night one of them had a nightmare and rushed out of his hut screaming and shouting as a result of the gramophone which had affected his brains. In his madness, he stumbled against a stone and fell cutting himself on the forehead. When he regained consciousness, he was bleeding freely. Akrofi was awakened, and dressed the wound, bathing it with potassium permanganate to stop the bleeding. In the morning the rest of the labourers asked their master not to use the machine again, else they would all go away. Akrofi agreed though not without reluctance; but not wanting his work to be interrupted, he agreed in the end and stopped playing the gramophone when the labourers were around.

As the plants grew, everybody had pleasure in looking at them. The leaves were large and beautiful. But, alas! Misfortune was at hand! The *akate* and other insects attacked the young trees mercilessly in their fourth year, when they had just started fruiting. The *akate* bit the branches and the sap oozed out, and the branches withered, and many of them died. The farm which at first wore a mantle of green now became brown, and dead leaves strewed the ground. In the meantime, the borer bored through many of the stems, and, in fact every person who passed there thought the whole farm would be destroyed.

At first, it was believed Akrofi managed his farms by the aid of a supernatural power for everything thrived; but at last the tide of success turned against him, and he was sorely disheartened. Some of the trees which had not yet been attacked by the *akate* or the borer began to wither, and he could not find the cause.

Many people advised him to abandon the farms, and leave the trees to their fate; for that is what many people do. As this advice was repeatedly given him by several of his friends, Akrofi was inclined to take it. But he considered the money he had spent on the farms, and the labour, so he decided to think twice. In the midst of his anguish, it flashed through his mind that he should consult the kind Curator at Aburi about his misfortune.

The orange, the pear and the other fruits trees were thriving, and his wife suggested they had better turn their attention to those, and leave the cocoa alone. In the meantime, the labourers worked the annuals — monkey-nuts, onions, etc. regularly and these yielded abundantly, and fetched sufficient money with which he was able to pay the labourers. But he was unwilling to abandon the cocoa which was supposed to be the chief of the cash crops[1] of the Gold Coast. He thought he would go to Aburi as stated above, but circumstances prevented him from doing so, and unfortunately, he could not write. Often he visited the farms, and found that no improvement was forthcoming. At last he made up his mind to go to Aburi where he could tell the Curator all what had befallen his farm, and to obtain advice from him.

---

[1] Text A and B both use rather awkward phrases here, so a modern term *cash crop* has been chosen instead.

The Easter rains had just started, which made travelling dangerous. As stated already there were no good roads and bridges. Therefore despite his anxiety about the condition of the trees in the farm, he could not possibly travel. The rains continued during April to July, and during August, they ceased. Having procured a few presents in the form of ivory knives, eggs, leopard skins, tiger[2] skins, monkey skins and python skins and groundnuts from his farm, he set out with five of his labourers for Aburi.

As you have already been informed, the road was impassable, more especially between Mpraeso and Anyinam. There was mud, knee-deep, and besides, there were swift-flowing rivers which no bridge spanned. The only means of crossing was provided by fallen trees, which were very slippery and dangerous to walk over. Yet, in spite of all these, Akrofi and his men travelled to Aburi to see the Curator.

Five days' journey brought them to Aburi. On the morning of the following day, they went to the Sanatorium and saw the Curator and his men hard at work. Greetings were exchanged, and as Akrofi could speak some Pidgin-English, he at once told him the reason for his visit.

"Sir," he began, "me I come again. I make fine plantation, I plant all trees you give me. The cocoa begin grow fine, but it spoil. Some small small animals e bite the trees, water from the trees dey come out. If I say I go catch the animal, e fall down quick. If I look, look, I no see am. This animal be plenty in my farm. Dey eat all the trees, they put plenty dust down. If I cut the tree to catch am, I see dey go up plenty that I must cut half of the tree away, and some times the tree fall down. Sometimes too, I no see the animal that bite the tree nor the one that live in the tree but I see that the leaves of some trees become red and fall down. So all my cocoa farm entirely spoil, I get debt plenty too much. People say I must leave the farm; some say

---

[2] There are of course no tigers in Africa, so Obeng is possibly referring to the serval cat.

I must work for some time. Me, I don't know what to do, so I come see you, and ask you what I must do."[3]

The Curator laughed and said: "I am sorry to hear all this. I will prepare some solution for you to spray the trees with to kill the 'small small animals' that bite. I will also show you how to kill the insects that live in the trees. Those trees which have not been attacked, but are withered, are being troubled by some insects from the ground that attack the roots. You must dig holes of about four or five feet radius around the trees, and in the holes, put in sufficient lime. It will kill all the insect which attack the roots, and the trees will grow healthily again. We used to have exactly the same troubles, but we have got rid of them. So do not worry. I will help you."

When the interpreter told Akrofi all what the man said, he was overwhelmed with relief and gratefully handed over the presents he had brought. The Curator accepted them with pleasure and gratitude. He then prepared the solution, and gave him a few sprayers and showed him how to use them. Akrofi remained at Aburi for three weeks, learning how to prepare the solution and how to spray.

The Curator instructed him to cut a piece of wire, like the rib of an umbrella, and sharpen the point, and thrust it into the holes in the stems of the trees where he would find dust. The wire would pierce through the grub and bring it out. In severe cases, he would have to cut the borer out, though as lightly as possible and stop up the hole with earth and tar. The Curator then asked Akrofi to let him know if the solution was successful or not. Before his departure, he gave him a further supply of seeds.

Akrofi, on his arrival, applied the solution freely, exactly as the Curator had instructed him. The rain troubled him a great deal, but he perservered in his work, remembering always the advice, which one day his European master at Obuasi had given

---

[3]   Obeng's rendition of Pidgin has been kept: spelling and all.

him that he should "take time in time, else the time be lost." Again people laughed at him, but he was, as usual, resolute.

He continued to do this work indefatigably, and gradually the trees began to show signs of good health. They flowered freely after the conquest of the enemies, and the root diseases, too, were defeated. The trees began to fruit again.

Drying frames and mats were prepared against the harvest. The pods were cut down and gathered in great heaps. A fermenting box had been made according to the direction of the Agricultural Officer. This was lined with plantain and banana leaves. The pods were then broken with small cudgels instead of knives, to avoid cutting through the beans. All mucilaginous matter was removed before the seeds were put on the drying frames. The sun shone brightly, and the seeds were stirred over and over at regular intervals. Because the seeds were fermented for six clear days, they looked very fine. When they were fully dried, the flat and imperfect beans were removed.

A broker, working with Messrs U.A.C. Ltd., heard of the excellent quality of the beans, and went there to buy. It was the first fruiting, so Akrofi did not get many loads, for almost every tree gave him from four to ten pods. At the end of the season, however, he had sold two hundred and fifty loads of sixty pounds each, and as there was no 'pool' among the European buyers, there was a keen competition amongst them, and Akrofi obtained very good prices.

Some other farmers whose farms were four or five times larger than Akrofi's, and who had many more trees in their respective farms than he, reaped much below the loads of Akrofi. Their trees were planted too closely together; some at four feet, others at three feet apart with the intention to kill the weeds when they grew. When the trees grew, they were slim and unhealthy, for they could not get sufficient air and plant food. These farmers became envious of Akrofi's success, and here again, they spoke ill against him, saying that he farmed with witchcraft. Akrofi could not say anything to convince or enlighten them.

In course of time, the orange, the kola, the coffee and all the other fruit trees began to fruit. The fruits were big and juicy, because he allowed all the oranges to ripen, whereas the children of his neighbours threw stones into the trees to pluck them before they ripened, with the result that they could not be sold. Akrofi, on the other hand, received orders from the District Commissioner and the miners in the neighbourhood, and his prosperity increased with leaps and bounds.

One morning, his wife expressed some desire for fish. Akrofi ordered one of his labourers to set a fish trap in the nearest stream, and sent some others to hang baited hooks across the water. Next morning they visited the traps and the hooks, and brought home a very good catch. One labourer suggested that in order to preserve a supply of fresh fish for his mistress, when she needed it, he would like to dig a hole and fill it with water, and put in the fish and feed them, so that any time the mistress wished to have a fresh fish, they simply had to bait a hook and catch some. This was a welcome suggestion, so the man and some of his friends, armed with spades and pick-axes, went to select a good site for the aquarium[4]. A deep and large rectangular pit was dug, and fish caught from the stream were put into it and fed. It was delightful to watch these young fishes eating. The intestines of animals killed, ants and fragments of food and many kinds of leftovers were chopped into pieces and scattered into the pit. The fish swam up and down the pit and darted upon these bits with all possible alacrity. In less than six months, they grew wonderfully big, and became fit to be eaten. This provided Akrofi and his wife with a pleasant change of diet. The poultry too grew and multiplied abundantly, as no hawks preyed on them. In fact they had more fowls than they needed, and the surplus was sold in the neighbouring villages.

The fruit trees were yielding abundantly, and pears, oranges, cocoa-nuts, kola nuts and all the different fruits were doing very

---

[4] What we today would call a 'fish pond'.

well, and more hands had to be engaged to carry these to the junction of the motor road whence they were carted into the trading centres for sale. The kola was sent to Lagos under the charge of his clerk, and was disposed of at Lagos city, Benin, Port Harcourt and other important towns. The market was good, especially for white kola.

The farms yielded so abundantly that in a few years Akrofi was the envy of all who neglected their farms and worked them by the "rule of thumb". He was able to send all his children to school, some continued in secondary schools and universities. As he himself was illiterate, he never omitted to express his regret over this, and he spared no money where the education of his children was concerned. They too worked very hard at their studies, and each year found them in a higher class. At the primary school, no other boy was able to compete with them, and they topped their respective classes until they passed the seventh standard. The eldest son, Sam, passed with distinction, and was granted a scholarship at the Prince of Wales School and College. This eased the burden of their father, therefore he was well able to look after the younger son at the same institution. Akrofi's children were not only intelligent, but their conduct, as commented upon by the Principal, was exemplary. Sam passed through the secondary school easily, and entered the University. Here too, he obtained a scholarship, and was sent to Oxford to complete his studies. His intelligence and good behaviour captivated the Masters there, and he was considered a model student. One day, one of his fellow students, who was rebuked by a Master because an African had surpassed him, spoke ill against Sam at their hall of residence, and said: "If you surpass me in spelling, you can never beat me in my white skin."[5]

---

[5] Obeng obviously knows little about university life. The British editors left this section out, but since the theme of racism appears here, it has been retained. What has been changed, though, is the reference to a hall of residence as a 'dormitory' and that the Master rebuked the other student for being surpassed by an African in 'spelling' (hardly a test likely to be used in a university).

Sam replied that "a white paper without black ink is useless". Some other collegians interfered and advised the British student to report the matter to his tutor. Sam was afraid, for he knew full well that the white people, unlike Africans, always supported their friends. When he was called to see his tutor, he had the heart of a hare, but outwards he put on a brave face. The matter was examined by the Hall authorities, who gave judgment in favour of poor Sam who was really trembling inwardly. Afterwards they all became very friendly and nothing occurred which showed that there was any open contempt of the African colour.

Sam continued there peacefully, and in course of time he successfully passed his exams and obtained the degrees of M. A. and B. C. L.[6] and was called to the Bar. He then embarked for Africa. On his arrival he obtained an appointment in the service of the Gold Coast Government as a District Magistrate at Osoroase.

On the evening of his departure to Accra for instruction, his father gave an 'At Home' in honour of his son's departure; and when the guests were assembled at the table, Akrofi made the following speech in his vernacular. He began:

"Gentlemen, it is not with a little pleasure that I invited you here this evening. Somewhere in the Good Book it has been written that we must rejoice with those that rejoice and weep with those that weep. This is not a matter of weeping, but of rejoicing. My son has completed his university course, and has obtained an appointment in the Government Service, hence we have met here to-night. Before my son leaves me to take up his high position, there is something I should like to tell him in your hearing. When the Sekondi–Kumasi Railway was being constructed, I went there as a labourer; but I did not like hard

---

[6] Obeng added a Diploma in Public Health here for good measure, but the British editors obviously thought the other qualifications more than enough.

work, so I left, leaving my wages for two months behind. I then came to Obuasi to find work with the Mining Company. After a short stay, I applied for permission to work in the pit, as that branch fetched much higher pay. We used to descend into the pit in a basket suspended by some chains. One night, at about ten o'clock, when one gang was going to relieve another, the chain broke, and the twenty-seven men in the basket died at once.

"I should have gone down with that batch, but, as it happened, a certain man had arrived from Kwahu, and I was talking to him when the hooter sounded. As the man had not finished speaking, and it was over three years since I left home, I could not leave him, and I decided to listen to him to the end. But as it was, my almost miraculous absence from work saved my life.

"The next day I reported that I could not continue working in the pit, though I was paid one shilling and sixpence per day, while those who worked at the top, that is, on the surface of the earth, received ninepence or one shilling. The General Manager was informed that I had shirked duty, and I was asked to appear before him at his office. I met him there with a fat cigar in his mouth and his hands in his pockets. He was also plump.[7] He spoke to me very harshly, saying that I must either continue working in the pit, or leave the mines, else I would make the rest of the labourers nervous. As I was afraid to go down the pit again, and as I had earned no money with which I could come home then, I simply said, 'Yes Sir,' and went away.

"I decided to remain in the house for some time, and then go to ask for some job elsewhere in the mines. I kept indoors for a fortnight, going out in the night like the owl. Then, under a false name, I approached the gardener of the mines, and

---

[7] Text B has omitted these two sentences describing the appearance of the General Manager

obtained a job. During that time I wished to save my wages; so I did not draw them, but foolish as I was, I asked my master to keep all for me. Unluckily, I began to be arrogant to my subordinate labourers, and treated them very unkindly, forgetting that pride goes before a fall. Sometimes I reported them to our master and they were fined or they were dismissed. Because of this, they plotted against me, and schemed to effect my downfall. They falsely accused me and repaid me in my own coin. The tide of my fortune turned. My master, who loved me, went to England on furlough, and a new master who did not know Joseph came to relieve him. Before he left Obuasi, he asked me to take all my money which he kept for me, but, not knowing what was coming, I asked the new master to keep it for me as before. I only retained five pounds to keep on me.

"The labourers renewed their conspiracy, but decided not to say anything to the white man. Instead, they reported to the General Manager that I was there under a false name. I knew nothing about these plans, of course. Then one morning, as we were working in the garden, I found that the labourers had divided themselves into various groups and all were talking and singing and laughing. In one of the their songs one man soloed: 'To-day be to-today,' and the rest chorused with the same words fortissimo. Another man said: 'By sunset somebody will see that in the cannon there is fire.' Another said 'In arrogance there is nothing but downfall.' I muttered to myself: 'Something is brewing.' In order to silence them, I made up my mind to separate them. I therefore called them individually and set them to different tasks; some were instructed to dig; others to fork, others to weed; others yet to mulch and others to prune. They all refused my orders for the first time. No one did what I told him. As you can imagine, I was very annoyed. I called their headman; but he told me openly that I should cease to bother him with my tyranny.

"They were still singing their songs, when my master's steward boy came to the garden. When the workmen saw the man they all shouted 'Hooooooi to-day be to-day. All trouble will end to-day and from this hour'. The steward boy walked up to me, and told me that his master wanted to see me at his office. I asked the boy what was the matter; but he would not tell me. I followed him there and then; and when I drew nearer to the office I knocked at the door, and was asked to go in. With a bow I greeted them; but only the General Manager responded. I then stood in silence. 'Ah, that's the man,' said the General Manager.

"My master then asked me, 'Have you worked at the pit before?'

"Err, err, where, Sir?"

"I say, have you worked in the pit at this mine before?"

"Yes, yes Sir. I came here once and I go home and come again."

"Did you work in the pit, blasting with dynamite when you were here at first?"

"No the one be my brother, he resemble me too much."

I then looked round the room, and drew nearer and nearer to the entrance door which was then standing ajar.

"Have you never worked at these mines before you came to be my gardener?"

"I coughed as if I was clearing my throat and said, 'I say I come here before I came to work for you, Sir."

"With what name did you work at first?" The General Manager interrupted.

"In my country I bear several nick-names, and those who knew me there used to call me anything they liked, Sir."

"Under what name are you working here now? Are you aware that in the garden where you work, some of the workmen come from your own country?"

I stood mum.

"If you don't speak, you will be put under arrest. I am the General Manager of these mines, and all the power is invested .n me, and I can do you anything I like, if you defy me."

"I then coughed again and drew nearer to the door and pretended to throw out the phlegm, and then I darted away.

"I left all my accumulated wages in the hands of my master. I could not go to my house to take my belongings, and through the bush I crawled and wandered day and night parallel with the Obuasi–Kumasi line, until after eight days' rambling in the bush, I was lucky enough to hit the main road to Kumasi from where I continued my journey through Juaben, Effiduasi, Kumawu, Agogo and on the Afram Plains to Abene and then arrived home as destitute and poor as I left home many years earlier. Because of this poverty, gentlemen, I pledged myself to Owusu Aduemiri for the paltry sum of eighteenpence, the value of the providential cutlass, which became the 'Open Sesame' that broke my hard luck and so firmly established me in this good stead as you all witness to-day.

"My advice which I wish to give to you, my son, to-day, is this: Remember always that those in high positions have many blasts to shake them, and, if they fall, they dash themselves to pieces. Do not be envious of fame, for it does not last long; nor of power, for it stings the hand that wields it; nor the gold, for though it glitters, it never glorifies. Choose rather love and justice and mercy, and hold them for ever in your heart of hearts. Love is the purest and mightiest force in the universe, and once it is yours, all other gifts shall be added on to you. Be merciful in all your judgments. Besides, envy not greatness for that rather makes the distance greater; always stoop to rise. Love not a person for his beauty neither abhor him for his outward appearance. Whatever income that you have, spend less. Shun corruption as you would a snake, for it has singed many hands that received it, and has dislodged many out of their positions and sent them to jail. But give all honour to truth and never sell it. Keep this short but pithy advice always in your mind before you assume your duties as a District Magistrate."

The young man was very moved; and with tears streaking on both cheeks, he vowed and promised faithfully to abide by his father's advice. The other gentlemen who were there said a few words in corroboration of all what Akrofi has said, and the assembly then dispersed.

CHAPTER 15

The Bounties of Mother Earth

AKROFI HAD grown from prosperty to prosperty, and so all his friends had deserted him. When he tried to go near them they shunned him as if they had seen a snake. He was not happy, for it was his nature to be sociable. In order to win back his friends, he made up his mind to bait them with generosity; but in this he did not succeed. Whenever he sent presents of any kind to them, some rejected them, and those who accepted them never gave any form of thanks or acknowledgement. When he inquired whether the presents reached them, some replied in the affirmative, and stated they were sorry that their boys whom they sent to thank him failed to run the errand. Those who rejected the presents stated that "the porcupine and the leopard do not rub tails together," meaning that they could not in any way reciprocate his kindness, therefore they could not acccept his presents. But as it was, Akrofi never expected any return whatsoever; but as hard as he tried to explain this to them, they never paid any heed to him. This pained Akrofi not a little, and so he made up his mind to withdraw himself from society.

He and his family and his workmen remained at the farm, quite contented and happy. His farms continued to flourish, and cocoa, fruits and food-stuffs of all kinds yielded so profusely that more and more hands were every now and then employed. More and larger houses were built to accommodate them. Many people who had been thrown out of work went there to find employment; and they were well treated and fairly and regularly paid, they always worked well and everybody believe that Akrofi's success was due to magic.

The farms were extended each year, and both annuals and

108

perennials were put in. The poultry increased rapidly and the fish pond swarmed with fish.

One day Akrofi felt to visit the workmen. He was accompanied by his wife, and they went round from one gang to another. They arranged to have lunch at the farm, so a servant carried their chop-box behind them. At noon they sat down under the canopy of the shade-trees and had their meal. His wife was tired and desired to have a siesta. Akrofi ordered the servant to run home for a camp-bed, but she preferred to lie on the dry leaves that had fallen from the trees. As she was dozing she felt that something was moving, or attempted to do so beneath her. To her horror she saw that she was lying on a snake, which was trying to crawl away form beneath her. With a scream she jumped as far from the place as possible. The couple then continued their rounds and reached where the men were digging. One of the newly engaged men could not handle the fork rightly to drive it in to the full length of the prongs, so Akrofi took hold of it and showed him how it should be done. When he drove it in at full depth, all at once the prongs stuck under a weight which he could not turn up, and when he used a little force, to lever it, two of the prongs got broken. A labourer told the man who was originally using the fork that he was lucky the fork did not get damaged when he was using it, else he would be asked to pay for it, and a deduction would be made from his wages. The other workmen laughed. Akrofi did not understand Hausa, so he could not understand why they were all laughing. He asked the headman, who told what they meant. Akrofi smiled and said he could not be so cruel as to fine a labourer who damaged a tool while working. He tried to lift up that weight, but he could not. Then he asked for a pick-axe and a spade and dug round it. He at first thought it was huge stone buried in there; but no, that was not the case. It was a huge jar with two handles which had been sealed firmly with sealing-wax. They also found that a chain had been passed through the handles and one end stuck in a thick odum tree standing a few yards off. The labourers did not know what it contained and why it was buried so deep. Akrofi and his wife knew that it contained pure gold, and so he asked the workmen to go home to rest and resume work the following day. He also instructed the headman to see that the men were employed at another part of the farm. Then he ordered them to bury the jar as deeply as before.

Akrofi and his wife returned home, where they ate some biscuits and drank a little wine and blessed their stars for their lucky discovery. When the workmen had gone to enjoy their half-holiday, the couple returned to the spot to see to the jar again for the woman was anxious to keep watch on the treasure. Later they returned home again, and Akrofi ordered that a fat and castrated sheep was to be slaughtered. The carcass was given to the workmen, and with the blood in a vessel, the couple went back to the place yet again. As was customary, they sprinkled the jar with the blood.[1] Then the decayed links of the chain were cut through with a chisel, and the heavy and precious jar was removed from its hidling place. Under the cover of darkness it was conveyed to the house, carried on a branch of raffia-palm to which it was tied, by four of the newly employed labourers who could not speak the Akan language.

Mother Earth had indeed repaid Akrofi amply for his industry! Akrofi, who sometime back was so poor as to pawn himself for eighteenpence, was now practically a millionaire! In the night, and in their chamber, the seal of the jar was broken, and gold nuggests and gold-dust and heavy trinkets streamed out of it. How bright and how beautiful it was! It was so much that the couple could not store it anywhere in their room. It was put back into the jar and the happy couple repeatedly blessed their stars for their lucky discovery.

One of the labourers greatly wondered why the blood of the sheep was carried away in a vessel, and inquired whether

---

[1] To appease the original owner of the hoard.

it was drunk raw by the master and his wife or it was intended for a special purpose. They spoke a lot about this amongst themselves, for some of the workmen had wished to have the blood for a blood-porridge. While they were talking about it, the headman approached, and heard that they were still speaking about the blood which was not given them for their own consumption. He knew where it was taken to, and why it was taken there, so he explained to them that it was not drunk by their master and mistress as they supposed, but it was poured over the big chained jar which they dug out. They wondered why the blood was sprinkled over the jar instead of being given to them for food. As hard as they tried, they could not understand it. As no other man was able to explain the real meaning to them, they left the matter alone.

In course of time, as a certain man wished to make a farm at the same place where Akrofi was farming, he went to see the Omanhene with the customary drinks. Some servants were sent to conduct the applicant to where Akrofi was, and to ask him to give a portion of the land to the applicant. The servants went with their luggage-carriers and after Akrofi had shown them the land in question, and everything had been completed, they returned home. Before they left the place, one of Akrofi's workmen asked one of the luggage carriers why blood is customarily poured over a jar dug out of the earth. That young man did not know the reason, so he failed to make the point clear to the inquirer. On their way home, that young man who failed to elucidate the point to the labourer asked one of the Ohene's servants why blood is customarily bespattered over a jar dug out of the ground. The man in turn asked the inquirer why he wanted to know what it meant. He told him that when they were at the village, one of Akrofi's servants asked him the meaning, but he had failed to explain it to him. On hearing this, the man was amazed, and asked the boy if he could identity the particular labourer who asked him that question. He told him that the man's name was Jatto Dagomba, and he could easily identify him. They then communed amongst themselves whether they should return to the village for further enquiries or not; but after much consideration, they decided to reach home and to report the matter officially to the Omanhene.

On their arrival they reported to the Omanhene that they had seen Akrofi and told him the Omanhene's errand, and in obedience to it, he had apportioned a land to the applicant; and that they had remained there for four days to demarcate the boundaries and to fix the boundary pillars. Akrofi had treated them very kindly and regaled them very sumptuously. They visited his farms and found for themselves that the land on which he was farming was very rich indeed. Akrofi had sent some fruits: oranges, white kola and pears and mangoes to the Omanhene. He had also sent some bush meat and some fish from his fish pond. The Omanhene received all these presents with grateful thanks.

In the evening, when the bath horn was blown to notify the public that the Omanhene was having his evening bath, the head of the messengers returned to the Palace and waited until all the servants who came to bathe him and donned him with his soft evening cloth had repaired to their houses. It yet remained child servants under ten years of age who had permission to go to the harem to invite that woman nominated by the Omanhene to come and pass the night with him. As custom forbade any full grown man to see the face of one of the Omanhene's wives, that man hastily asked permission to speak to him.

He began by explaining that when they went to Akrofi's village, they heard that he had killed a sheep and carried the blood to a corner of his farm where he bespattered it over a big jar which he had dug out of the ground and brought home. The Omanhene then inquired from the servant whether the information was correct and whether they could name and identify their informant should Akrofi repudiate and deny the charge. The Omanhene being assured of these facts, they were still debating as to what steps they should take to trace the jar, when they heard the young servants who had gone to the harem crying: "Turn about! Get away from sight, everybody! She is coming O! Kneel down and cover your face!" Even in the darkness these were the warnings given to the public, indicating that a King's wife was passing and no other eye was to see her. That being the case, the Omanhene ordered the man to leave the Palace at once and to see him again early the next morning.

Whether that man slept in the night or not, the story does not tell, but he rose so early that he was at the Palace before dawn. As soon as the departure of the Omanhene's wife was reported, he requested an audience. The Chief Linguist was sent for and it was arranged that somebody should be sent for Jatto Dagomba, who had divulged the information. Two servants were sent out at once, and two days later Jatto stood before the Omanhene. He was asked to narrate to them all what he knew in connection with the sheep which Akrofi had killed about a couple of weeks ago. Jatto, not knowing the importance of his statement, told them all what he saw and heard and said the blood was carried in a vessel by their headman who went with Akrofi and his wife, and sprinkled all over a big jar which was carried home. He was asked to mention the name of the headman who carried the jar to Akrofi's house; and he said his name was Ali Bazamberimi and his assistant was Majida Mamprusi. Messengers were sent to ask Akrofi to allow these two men to come to see the Omanhene, and in the meantime, Jatto Dagomba was detained.

The Omanhene drank and played, but he was thinking and his 'eyes became red'[2], for he recalled events of the past. He stated that when a great war was about to break out between Ashanti and his State, the then Omanhene collected all the gold dust and nuggets and trinkets forming the regalia and the paraphernalia and put them into four big jars. These were chained

---

[2] This Akan reference to anger does not appear in Text B.

to trees at different places so that they might be easily traced after the war and recovered. Unluckily, the Ashantis defeated Kwahu and ransacked the Palace and searched the bush for booty. It was believed they had removed all the precious jars, for just after the war, the treasurers were sent out in search of them, but they could not find where the fourth was buried, and therefore it was assumed that it too had been removed by the enemy. Now it was established, that this fourth jar which, according to tradition, was the largest and contained the most valuable treasure and had been chained to an odum tree, had been discovered by Akrofi. Therefore if it could be proven that Akrofi had the possession of it, he would be very severely dealt with. The messengers had to swear that they would never divulge the cause of their mission to anybody.

The couriers arrived at Akrofi's village in less than two days, and on the third day, both Ali Bazamberimi and Majida Mamprusi stood before His Majesty and answered questions regarding the discovery of that jar. They did not know what was behind the screen of the mind of the potentate and his assemblage, so they openly related all about the jar and all what happened at the village. The Omanhene then found that the information was correct, and sent for the Adontenhene, and with him he arranged to send for and to arrest Akrofi and his wife. Later it was ordered that the woman should not be arrested, but should be served with a summons, for she was the only person who witnessed the exhumation of the jar besides the headman, and she had additionally been present when it was opened.

The new messengers quickly departed for the village. But when they saw Akrofi, because of his dignity, they could not put him under arrest. As soon as they arrived, he regaled them sumptuously and gave them the best of treatment, asked them the object of their visit, and inquired after the two labourers whom the Omanhene had summoned to his capital. They did not reply to this, but stated that the Adontenhene had sent them to invite him, so he should prepare to start with them early the next day.

Akrofi told them he was so busy that he could not accompany them at once, for owing to the depletion of his hands, he had to lend a helping hand to the rest of the labourers. He was told that whether he had time or not, he must accompany them, for if he refused, a much hardier messenger would be sent to force him to go. He inquired whether any summons or criminal charge had been preferred against him, but they told him they could not say.

Akrofi went in to tell his wife all what had happened; and she told him that the detention of the two labourers by the Omanhene had led her to think that the discovery of the jar had been divulged in the capital. She therefore advised Akrofi that before they left the farm, he should rebury the jar with all its contents, so that they could deny all knowledge of it should they be questioned about it. She added that as some of the labourers saw that it was brought to their house, a fragment of a broken jar which was also dug out at another part of the farm by a member of another gang, should be brought instead of the precious one. They knew that according to the custom of the country, anybody finding a treasure-trove was to send it full to the Ohene of his town, who in turn would send it to the Omanhene. As they had failed to do so, they knew fully well that they would lose the case.[3]

It was arranged that their youngest son should go with lightning speed to Osoroase to report the whole incident to their son, Sam, the District Magistrate, and to ask him to prepare for their defence, should they be criminally charged. In fact, both husband and wife were highly disturbed, but they showed outward calm. That night, through the back entrance, both of them stole away under cover of darkness, into the remote corner of their large farm where they buried the precious jar and all what it

---

[3] It is in view of this knowledge of custom, that Akrofi's subsequent winning the case against the Omanhene in the colonial High Court in Accra, is difficult to understand.

contained. They scattered decayed leaves and dead branches over the disturbed ground, and then they stealthily crept home like thieves. Before the light was put out, Akrofi told his wife that they had made a great mistake, so he wished to go and bring the jar back to the house, for he felt that, insignificant as they were, they should be proud of their good name. Though the woman said many things to discourage Akrofi not to do so, he was resolute. He lit his lantern and with a shovel and a pick-axe in his hand he returned to the spot alone, dug the jar out once more, and came home with it. They sealed it up again, exactly as it was found, and it was put in a room securely locked.

Early the next morning, the couple were the first to awake; for the previous night, liquor had been lavished on the King's servants. About half past six, the servants of the King took their bath and then breakfasted. On the point of their departure, some more drinks were served and all the people at the farm were invited to partake. Akrofi was then marched to the capital, a prisoner at large, followed by his wife. Of course, as she was a witness in the case, she was, according to the native custom, separated from her husband, and no communication whatever was allowed between them.

After a hard and toilsome march, the messengers arrived with their esteemed prisoner. He was not handcuffed because of his dignity; for everybody knew that Akrofi would never attempt to escape to disgrace himself. The following morning, he was committed to trial on a charge of having kept for himself a treasure which he dug out of the King's forest without bringing it to the Ohene to claim his share, according to custom.

When he was asked to make a statement, he said that the value of the jar of gold exceeded one hundred thousand pounds, so he believed the case could not be tried by the Native Admin-istration Ordinance. The case was therefore transferred to the District Commissioner's Court where it was likely that his son, the young Magistrate could plead for him.

CHAPTER 16

The Trial of Akrofi Before the District Commissioner

AKROFI WAS arraigned before the District Commissioner on a charge of having dug out a treasure in a jar which was the bona fide property of the Kwahu Stool, and of having kept it for himself without bringing it to the Omanhene and claiming his share.

When the charge was put before the District Commissioner and the Registrar asked Akrofi his plea, the Districct Commissioner stated that a case involving a sum of one hundred thousand pounds could not be tried by his court; it was therefore transferred to the High Court to be tried by His Lordship the Chief Justice of the Gold Coast Colony and its Dependencies.

There were many cases already on the Chief Registrar's list and as the charge was not criminal in the sight of British Law, Akrofi was allowed to remain at large. After the disposal of some of the old cases, Akrofi was called before the Judge to explain his case. He was not bound by any Criminal Law, so the Judge asked him not to retain the services of any lawyer, but to make his own statement, for the local lawyers charged exorbitant fees, especially in cases involving large sums of money as Akrofi's did.

Akrofi stated that he bought[1] a piece of land on which he

---

[1] There are many inconsistancies in this part of the book. This is for instance the first time we hear of Akrofi actually having bought the land he is farming. The reader's reaction might therefore be that Akrofi is lying. Later, however, the author makes 'damage control' and lets the appropriate papers etc. be brought.

farmed, and when he was digging a part of the farm, he dug out a jar. According to custom, he sprinkled blood on it and brought it home. Before he had time to report this discovery to the right persons, he was arrested and brought before the Omanhene. Without any investigation, he was at once committed for trial. At the Court of the Native Tribunal he stated that the Tribunal had no jurisdiction over a case involving a sum of hundred thousand pounds, and so it was transferred to the British Court.

His Lordship said if he bought the land on which the treasure was found, then, in the sight of British Law, he could not find any reason why he was to be charged with stealing and tried. A letter was sent to the Omanhene to inquire whether the land was really sold to Akrofi or not. The Omanhene replied that Akrofi did not buy the land, but it was given to him freely as a citizen of the State; and in such circumstances, every citizen who discovered any treasure, had to present this intact to the Ohene of the State.

Akrofi was again called and charged with having given a false statement. It now appeared that the first case had been put aside; for Akrofi now had to prove to the satisfaction of the court that he had bought the land. Akrofi therefore asked the permission of the Judge to retain the services of a barrister, which was granted. He also wished his son, the District Magistrate, to come to his aid, but being a Government Official, holding the Office of a District Magistrate, the Colonial Secretary decreed that he could not take any professional part in the case. This baffled Akrofi not a little, for though he could receive advice from his son, he could not render professional advice in a professional capacity. A newly arrived barrister having been consulted, Akrofi decided to retain him. His name was William James Akotua, M.A; LL.B; PhD.[2] He asked Akrofi for a retaining fee of two

---

[2]   Again the author has in Text A given an even longer string of qualifications, something that obviously interested Obeng a lot. The present editor has, however, decided to stick to the professional assessment of Text B.

hundred and fifty pounds as preliminary fee, which was paid at once.

The new lawyer gave Akrofi every assurance that he would win the case for him, adding that if his client were brought to trial about the jar, he would win that case too. Lawyer Akotua had recently arrived from England, where he had studied at Lincoln's Inn, and was a holder of many credentials testifying to his expertise in the Criminal Law. He had practised for three years in England without losing a single case. There was no better person to handle Akrofi's case.

The Omanhene's representative arrived in Accra and retained the services of a Lagosian barrister whose name was Okuola. He too was a well qualified lawyer for he had the same string of degrees as Akotua.

When the day came for the hearing of the case, both lawyers appeared in court to display their ability and eloquence. Barrister Okuola, the prosecuting lawyer, opened the case and addressed the Judge and the court as follows:

"My Lord, and gentlemen of the Jury! It is well known in every corner of this Colony that in the days of yore, the Ashantis were very aggressive. They waged unlawful wars against peaceful people and states, such as the Kwahu State. Because of their power and skill in warfare, every State fell before them. This continued until the year 1826, when all the Amanhene and principal chiefs along the Coast, assisted by the British Government, defeated King Osei Yaw at Akantamansu during the month of August. His Golden Stool was nearly captured by the enemy, but the brave King of Juaben, Nana Boaten Akuamoa fought with the bravery of a lion and recaptured it for him. As it is, there is no person at this court, who has not had an ancestor killed in one of these bloodthirsty Ashanti wars. Yet the Ashantis themselves believed that they always had a reason and gave a warning of an impending attack, if need be. There is not a single State in this country which has not been attacked. Because of this, well-to-do persons used to bury all their treasures to avoid their being taken by these greedy and troublesome Ashantis. It was, in those day, that the proverbial saying: 'tame and simple as a Kwahu man', was coined for a person who was gentle and taciturn.

"Since time immemorial, the people in this State have been very enterprising. Some are very good hunters and sharp-shooters, killing elephants, buffaloes, the rhinoceros and the hippopotamus and a great deal of other big game. They used to remove the heavy ivory tusks, and share these with their Kings. Some of them were good farmers who grew all kinds of foodstuffs, and made a lot of money. Others were cloth-weavers and wove beautiful native cloths which outlived the present European cotton cloths for tens of years. Some were potters and made utensils, and occasionally modelled the images of demised Kings and Chiefs which they sold for large sums of money. Others were fishermen, and in their rivers, in the Afram and in the Volta and their tributaries, they caught large quantities of fish which they sold. Some were basket and mat-weavers, others yet were snail-gatherers, and they too earned good money. Because the subjects were so industrious and thrifty, it is obvious that their Kings were very rich.

"The ancient Amanhene were indubitably wealthy. They possessed many gold trinkets, bangles of heavy weight; headgears with gold amulets and gilded gourds, gold sandals, finger rings for every finger; wrist and calf amulets of massive gold and above all a large Gold Stool, all made with solid gold. Your Lorship, at the rumour of war, fearing that the Ashantis would suddenly attack them and capture these treasures by surprise, and rob the royal treasury of all it possessed, the wise Omanhene of that time bought four large jars into which he put all the treasures in the Palace, including the gold dust and nuggets, all the regalia and paraphernalia, court-criers' caps, soul-washers' breast-plates, linguists' sticks, and so forth. Deep holes were then dug into which these jars, with their valuable contents, were buried. Your Lordship, to mark the places of burial, thick chains were run through the handles of each jar, and the chains stuck into trees. Sometimes some of the treasures were buried at the bed of a diverted stream, and the chains only marked the place of burial. In thick and primeval forests, such valuable things were buried.

"One of these jars, your Lordship, is to have been dug out by the accused. According to custom, anyone who discovers such a treasure has to baptise it with blood before it is exhumed; after which it is sent to the Omanhene through the Ohene of the finder. In the present case it was to be sent through the Adontenhene. Akrofi knows this custom very well, your Lordship, and so his failure to follow it is a very heinous offence.

"These your Lordship, are the facts of the case, and I feel that your Lordship's experience and ability will lead to a prompt decision against the accused, whose offence in endeavouring to steal from the Omanhene this jar and its precious contents is without precedent in the annals of the Kwahu State. I have no doubt that your Honour has been well convinced, and like Daniel, you are ready to pronounce the right judgment."

He then sat down among the tremendous cheer of the people in the court who were much impressed by his eloquence and good knowledge of Gold Coast history.

His Lordship then made an effort to speak, but before he did so, barrister William James Akotua, rose to his feet, bowed and asked His Lordship's permission to speak. When it was granted, he said:

"Your Lordship and gentlemen of the Jury, I must crave your patience. I am not here to spin yarns and prattle and babble to waste the precious time of your Lordship and the people at the court as my learned friend has done. From what he said, I gather that he has laid all his facts before you. It yet remains that witnesses will prove the certainty of the facts he presented to the court.

"There are only two points, which I wish to bring to your Lordship's attention. First, my client has informed me that he bought the land from the Stool, so it is his with all what it contains by right of purchase. Second, my learned friend told the court that the jar in question contains gold dust, nuggets, and all the regalia and paraphernalia, court-criers' caps; soul-washers' breast-plates, linguists' sticks, trinkets, bangles, head-gears, sandals, finger-rings, amulets, guilded gourds and above all a Gold Stool made of massive gold which he described as large. These facts must be supported with evidence, personal and documentary, in order that your Lordship may arrive at a decision.

"The two points which I want to drag out are: First, if the land was legally sold and Akrofi bought it legally, then that land with all that it contains is his by the right of purchase. Secondly, the jar in question is to be brought to this court as an exhibit. If your Lordship opens the jar, and it is found that it contains all the articles which my learned friend so eloquently enumerated, then there is no doubt that it belongs to the Stool and as such, the jar with all its contents has to be given to the Paramount Chief. If the jar does not contain these articles, then the jar with its contents will go to Akrofi undivided."

Barrister Okuola consulted the Omanhene's representatives and readily gave his full assent to these terms.

His Lordship then ordered that evidences in support of the legal sale and purchase of the land on which the jar was exhumed were to be produced, as, in his opinion, these would easily settle the whole case.

Barrister Okuola then stated that Akrofi applied to the Omanhene for permission to farm on the land, but it was never sold to him. The servants of the Omanhene who went to inspect the land in question and cut the boundaries for Akrofi were mentioned, and they were ordered to be ready to be sworn as witnesses.

Akrofi was asked if he had any evidence supporting the legal sale and purchase of the land. He replied in the affirmative. He was asked to mention or produce them. He said that his evidence was documentary, and it was with his lawyer.

At this point the case was adjourned until the next day.

When the court resumed its sitting, the witnesses for the prosecution were called in support of Barrister Okuola's statement. Lawyer Akotua then cross-examined the principal witness as follows:

"Do you know the person to whom every land in this State belongs?"

"Yes."

"Tell the court his name and title."

"Akuamoa, the Omanhene of Kwahu."

"Do you know how long it is since Akrofi applied for permission from the Omanhene to farm on the land?"

"Yes."

"It was in what year?"

"I am not an educated man, so I cannot give you the year, but according to the number of farms Akrofi has made, I can calculate it to be about ten or eleven years."[3]

"Very good. Do you remember if there has been any change of rulers during the period?"

"Yes."

"What change?"

"One Omanhene in whose time the land was given to the man died, and another was installed in his place."

"Very well, thank you. Is the ruling monarch of this State despotic or constitutional?"

"I do not understand what you mean."

"I mean to say, has the ruling monarch of this State the power to do anything he pleases without any opposition, or is there another power that can oppose and correct him if he goes wrong?"

"Though the Omanhene is the 'All-powerful' in the State,

---

[3] Obeng's sequence of time is obviously not carefully calculated. We know he already has a son, Sam, who is a Magistrate. Since we were told that in 1913, all he possessed was a dog, from where did his adult children emerge?

yet in his capital he has some elders, including the Queen-Mother, who can correct, oppose or depose him, if he does not obey them."

"Very well. And in the State?"

"In the State too, his principal adviser, corrector, and everything is the Adontenhene. He is the Omanhene's right hand; and even in some cases, it appears that he has control over the Omanhene."

"What do you mean by 'in some cases it appears that he has control over the Omanhene'?"

"I mean to say there are some State ceremonies which the Omanhene cannot possibly perform without the Adontenhene."

"Give us some examples."

"At the annual Yam Festivals, it is the Adontenhene who puts mashed yam three times into the mouth of the Omanhene before he gets permission to eat some of the new yams."

"Is that all?"

"No. Every gin which will be poured over the ancient stools must be handled and blessed by the Adontenhene before it becomes sacred for the use of the spirits of the departed chiefs. At least it was so in the ancient times."

"Is that all?"

"Besides when the stools are to be sanctified annually, in the stream, the Omanhene cannot perform the ceremony unless the Adontenhene is present, and when at times he hesitates, or shows reluctance to be present, precious presents are lavished on him to persuade him to come."

"You are leading us astray from our main point, Barrister Akotua", interrupted the Chief Justice. "Ask questions which are helpful to the case before us."

"I must crave your Lordship's patience. These questions are by no means without bearing on the case as will shortly be clear." Akotua turned to the witness again. "When the land was presented to Akrofi to farm on it, was the Adontenhene informed?"

"Decidedly."

"Do you think the stool elders in the capital, including the Queen-Mother, know something about the presentation?"

"The Omanhene could not present the land without their knowledge."

"Very well. But if the Omanhene wished to sell the land, could he do so with or without their knowledge?"

"Any sale of land without the knowledge or permission of these people is not legal."

"And if it is sold with their knowledge and consent?"

"Then it is legal, and cannot be disputed."

"This is enough. That's all I want. Thank you."

Barrister Akotua then told the Chief Justice that the case had been settled. He then opened his hand-bag, and from it he pulled an old envelope, from which he took out a Document, which he handed to the Judge.

It read as follows:

"WHEREAS Akrofi appealed to us, four years ago, for a piece of land to farm on

"AND WHEREAS at first the land was given to him freely because he is a free citizen of his State,

"AND WHEREAS he has farmed extensively and it appears to us that he has become the possessor of the land now in his hands.

"NOW THEREFORE we the undersigned think it expedient to transfer the land to him by sale; and from this day onward, the land extending from a point on the right bank of the River Odihun southwards to the Odum Tree, meaning 9,756 feet more or less, and from the said Odum tree to the Wawa Tree in the easternly direction, meaning 8,687 feet more or less; and from the Wawa Tree running northwards to an Abako Tree, meaning 8,596 feet more or less and from the Abako Tree running westwards to the point on the bank of the River Odihu, measuring 9,876 feet more or less has become the bona fide property of the said Akrofi, his successors and assigns. We have received from the said Akrofi the sum of five thousand and seven pounds in full payment of the said land, and no other person whatever has any right to dispute his ownership of the land. The land has been sold with the consent and concurrence of the Adontenhene of Kwahu, the Queen-Mother, the Krontihene, the Akyeamehene and the Gyaasehene. This sale and purchase is therefore complete in its entirety and cannot be defied or altered or gainsaid by any of our successors. Dated at Abene in Akuamoa Panin Fie, this tenth day of September in the year of our Lord 1918, in the second year of our reign.

Akuamoa Mensah ....Omanhene of Kwahu
Amma Agyeiwaa .... Queen-Mother of Kwahu
Kwaku Amamfo .... Akyeamehene of Kwahu
Kwaku Anim .... Krontihene of Kwahu
Ado Kese Pambou .... Adontenhene of Kwahu

> Writer and Witness to Marks,
> James Benjamin Tie-agya-asem
> Tribunal Registrar of the Paramount Stool of Kwahu."

The Judge having read this document, asked Barrister Okuola whether his client was a true representative of the Omanhene of Kwahu. He replied that he was really the accredited representative of that Omanhene. He then asked Barrister Akotua to produce the jar in question as the second exhibit. Akrofi told the court that he had left the jar at home, and begged that some trustworthy men might be sent to fetch it in evidence.

Akintola Chipalsi, the Senior Superintendent of Police with a police sergeant and six constables were ordered to bring the jar within three days, as no more time could be spent on the case.

In the afternoon of the third day, the jar, the famous jar, was produced in court. The sight of the jar baffled everybody who had been at the court hearing the arguments on both sides. It was dirty, the size was about the thigh of medium sized person, and it was quite obvious that the articles enumerated by Lawyer Okuola could not have been put in it, for the neck was only eight inches wide. It contained some gold dust and nuggets, but none of the regal regalia previously mentioned.

The judge read the document about the sale and purchase of the land to the court and asked the plaintiff if he knew the persons who signed the document. He replied that they were real persons who occupied the Stools in whose connection they were mentioned, and so he knew that he had lost the case. Judgement was then pronounced in favour of Akrofi and against the ruling Omanhene and his people, and Akrofi thus became the sole owner of the area mentioned in the document His lawyer was well paid, and Akrofi and his wife returned to their village happy and contented.

CHAPTER 17

Attraction of Cohesion[1]

AKROFI HAD won his case, and had become the bona fide owner of the whole area mentioned in the document, signed and given him by the Omanhene. For his victory, praises were showered on Barrister Akotua. His opponent Barrister Okuola then vanished not only from the court like vapour before the sun, but from the town, like a ghost at the first cockcrow. The prosecution who had expected to win something from the case, and had therefore drained off all their wealth for Okuola in whom they had put all their trust, were distraught and angry. Lawyer Akotua told those who thronged at the entrance of the court like bees around the hive, that truth always shines as a fixed star and is as unbreakable as iron. Akrofi's enemies continued abusing and rebuking Okuola saying his exaggerated speech had lost the case. Others said that he was charmed or intimidated by the opposing party, else he would not have said that a gold stool, a linguist's stick, a crown, sandals etc. were all enclosed in the narrow necked jar, for that part of the speech spoilt the case.

Akrofi's wife was still in the witnesses' room when the judgement was pronounced; and when she heard the great noise following the judgement, she unconsciously asked: "Who run?" "Your enemies", was the quick reply. She then danced like a flower in the wind. The anguish and weariness that had preyed upon her mind disappeared. She became as happy as waves that dance on the sea.

---

[1] Text B has chosen the title of this chapter as: 'THE MAGNET OF SUCCESS'.

The land Akrofi won by the judgment was large and well selected. Many rivers traversed it, and so it was deep and fruitful. Because of his increased wealth, he was able to increase his farms. By the judgment of the court, all the gold contained in the famous jar became his bona fide property by right of purchase. Akrofi was asked to submit his bill of costs, but considering that the verdict had restored to him his freedom and his good name, he preferred to pay his costs himself.

Many people who were indebted went to him, and as domestic slavery was then not suppressed entirely,[2] Akrofi purchased the freedom for many of them; and by letting them work for him at reduced wages, they paid back the money in this way, the difference in pay being the return of the purchasing price, by instalments. His village grew larger and larger, and in course of a short period, it became a large town. People who belonged to the same clan as Akrofi's went there with their children, grand-children and dependents, and claimed kinship with him. Some said they were his brothers, others his nephews, others again his cousins, others grandsons, though in reality he had no blood-relative, not a single soul. His wealth, like a strong and powerful magnet, drew all these people to him; and Akrofi, who years back, was as poor as a church rat, and was compelled to pawn himself for the sum of eighteenpence, now became a veritable Croesus.

He had been poor before in the right sense of the word, and therefore he was very compassionate with the poor people. Those who were indebted, the sick, the forsaken, those in any kind or shape of trouble, appealed to him for help and assistance. Moreover, he knew full well, though illiterate himself, that he owed his present good fortune to education. It was the document signed and delivered by the Omanhene and those in authority that had saved him from the deep mine of infamy. Besides, through the insight and forethought of his lawyer, he was cleared

---

2   This is a very interesting piece of historical information removed from Text B.

of the charge of theft preferred against him. He therefore showed great love and kindness to the teachers and schoolmasters as well as all the Mission agents engaged in teaching. He was also eager to help children who had nobody to look after them at school[3], for as already stated above, he felt his illiteracy very keenly. He instituted funds for scholarships for children who showed ability in particular trades, such as carpentry, masonry, tailoring and shoe-making. He knew that mere reading and writing without good behaviour gave no credit; therefore when schoolmasters praised a boy or girl, for his or her good behaviour and patience, he was very highly pleased. He often said that patience must be compared to a sweet-scented flower, but as it takes a long time to bloom, very few persons have it in their gardens. If a child was not too bright, but was patient, he used to pay great heed to him. Once he said that the brightest diamond is often found in the darkest mud.

He respected most people who were not very clever. "Clever people," he once said, "are apt to deceive, and so can never be trusted. Because of their cleverness they are able to commit any kind of crime, and shelter themselves behind sugar-coated words and excuses which agree with the law. If a clever lawyer or magistrate cross-examines them, they escape by means of lies and deceit. Often they continue their evil career for years before falling into the pit they have dug for themselves."

Akrofi's fame flashed from lip to lip and town to town till he became well known in the whole Colony. His workmen were well treated and well paid. As they were extremely happy, they never wished to leave. They married and brought up their families in the locality, and in due course, Akrofi began to feel that the many children in his town should be given some sort of training.

One night, on a bright moon-lit night, he and his wife went for a stroll in the town, and saw many of the women clapping their hands, singing and dancing. Children of both sexes were

---

[3] In Ghanaian parlance: 'pay their school fees'.

wandering about playing hide-and-seek under the gaze of their parents. The next day he asked one of the labourers why he allowed his children to roam and play about in the night, and he replied that by that they got strength. Akrofi pointed it out to him that the habit was both dangerous and demoralising for the children. Something must be done. Akrofi made up his mind to make an evening school for the children.

A certain man, whose name was Odiasempa, presented himself as retired schoolmaster and applied for the post of head-master. He was offered two hundred and forty pounds[4] a year.

A temporary shed was made of bamboo; and when it was furnished, the teacher asked him to send for the necessary books and other materials. The children were freely supplied with books and other materials; but the teacher ordered that if any child lost or damaged a book or slate, he was to pay double the original price. The children looked after their materials with all possible care. Nearly every father sent a boy or girl to join, and in a short time seventy-two had been enrolled.

Akrofi appealed to the Mission School Supervisors for more teachers, but he was not assisted. He therefore appealed to the Government through the Adontenhene, who obtained the per-mission of the Omanhene to write to the Education Department about the new school and ask for a teacher. An Inspector of Schools was asked to go and inspect and report on the efficiency of the school before it was admitted on the Assisted List.

The Inspector arrived and saw the school in a topsy-turvy condition. As Akrofi was himself an illiterate, he was easily deceived. The Headmaster, who pretended to be a retired school-master, had only been a cook to a European headmaster. He

---

4   Text B suggests that the 'headmaster' was offered seventy-two pounds a year. Obeng knew the salary scales in the teaching service well, so the salary mentioned in Text A was not put there through ignorance. The figure most likely indicated a top salary in the Government Teaching Service, and because Akrofi 'did not know any better', he agreed to pay this very high salary.

could therefore speak English somehow, but could not read nor write a single letter of the alphabet. So he only pretended to be teaching. All what he was able to teach the children was 'Broken English'[5]. The children were so able to mention some articles in English and say a few sentences. That was all. They could not decipher a letter or a figure. They only drew lines on their slates and in their books, which of course had no meaning. Several exercise books had been filled in and kept in the school cupboard. On the arrival of the Inspector these were removed from the cupboard and put on a table for his inspection. Just at that juncture, the so-called headmaster told the Inspector that he had left a book at home and was going for it. With this excuse, he darted off like an apparition seen and gone, never to return.

When the Inspector had tested the children's knowledge of English, he asked the Senior boy to show him the exercise books. To his utter astonishment, he only saw that lines and circles and wavering lines had been drawn in all the books, but no writing. Nothing else had been done.

Akrofi told him how much he had spent on the teacher's salary and in purchasing school materials. The Inspector sympathised with Akrofi, and told him he would tell the Director of Education of his gallant efforts and recommend that a trained Government teacher should be put in charge of the school.

When this information reached the Director, he was highly pleased, and at once sent an able teacher to go and take charge at that school. A very good and sure foundation was laid by that energetic teacher, and the children progressed rapidly. They were taught to read and write and count, and were taught songs, how to play new games and how to draw, and soon a noticeable change was visible. There was no longer any running about at night; for the children slept at the right time.

---

[5] Obeng uses the word 'colloquial' here, whereas Text B uses 'very faulty'. Neither term is appropriate to the Ghanaian situation. 'Broken English' has therefore been chosen as a substitute.

Six months later, when the same Inspector came there again, great was his joy to see the striking change which had taken place. Akrofi promised to bear all the expenses of the school except the pay of the teacher. Therefore the School Inspector recommended that it should be placed on the Assisted List. More teachers were employed with the rise in the number on the roll, and before long the school was extended to Standard VII. Many applicants came there from different parts of the State, and Akrofi and his people fed them freely and sumptuously. Later, the children were asked to buy their own books, but Akrofi paid for the lighting and the sports material.

Those boys who were successful at the Seventh Standard Certificate Examination were either employed by the Government or the mercantile firms. Akrofi considered how those who failed could be made useful. The headmaster suggested they should be taught some handycraft. The Director of Education was consulted, and he endorsed their suggestion, and a well qualified handycraft master was appointed to augment the staff. A temporary house was built with wattle and mud and was thatched. Benches were made, and the Director supplied all the tools. As canes were abundant, the teacher taught them how to make any kind of cane-work — basket-chairs, tables and what not. These were sold and more tools and materials were purchased. But naturally, some of the boys did not like that work. They hated going to the bush, especially on wet days, for cane, and even if they went, they brought very little back.

One day, one of the boys, after he had been warned several times not to do so, came home with a small bundle, and made fun of another boy who brought a bigger bundle. This of course was reported to the handycraft teacher, who, as you can imagine, was greatly annoyed. He cut a piece of the lazy boy's cane into two, and with one piece, he whipped the boy beyond the limit.

The boy bled freely, and the remaining boys ran in all directions, shouting, and screaming. They reported the cruelty of their teacher to their parents. These came to report the case to Akrofi who was now looked upon as the chief of that town. He quickly ran to see the boy whom he found in a very helpless state. Luckily, a stranger who was selling drugs and chemicals had called some time ago, and a bottle of iodine permanganate had been bought for seven shillings and sixpence[6] and this was at once applied to the wounds. The oozing of the blood was suppressed and iodoform ointment was applied and in less than a couple of weeks, the boy was quite well again.

The teacher was brought before Akrofi, and with the help of the headmaster, the case was amicably settled. As you can imagine, the boy was blamed and rebuked for laziness and bad behaviour and strongly warned that such conduct should never be repeated. They told him that 'since laziness travelled so slowly, poverty soon overtook him'. Those parents who had thought that the teacher would be found guilty and be dismissed were surprised at the decision.

After they had dispersed, Akrofi called the teacher and the headmaster and severely reprimanded the teacher. He pointed out to him that such cruelty and brutality was rampant among the teachers of the seventeenth century, but in these enlightened days, such a case would have been an offence to be brought before a magistrate had it been reported to the police. Both the head-master and the teacher expressed great gratitude for the kindness and generosity of Akrofi, and the offender vowed with tears on his cheeks, that he would never allow his temper to conquer him again. The headmaster told the teacher that when he was a boy, his teacher had taught him a couplet which he had never forgotten and which was his daily companion. It ran:

"Before you speak a hasty word, count ten;
And, if you still angry be, count again."

---

6 Obeng was very business minded, and we see frequent references to prices and amounts of money in his work.

The teacher again thanked the headmaster and repeated that he was truly sorry for his hasty action. Akrofi then said:

"When I was working at Obuasi as headman of the gardeners, I used to chastise my subordinates almost in the same way as you did. Once I flogged a boy who bled freely, and as a result of his loss of blood, he fainted. Different types of medicines, African and European, were tried, but all in vain. At long last, when all hope was lost, and it was believed the boy had died, a native physician, who charged thirteen shillings as his preliminary fee, was consulted, and he promised to restore him to consciousness. He threw plenty of dry pepper and some amount of guinea grain into a receptacle, and put live coals on it. It produced a thick fume of smoke, over which he held the boy upside down with his nostrils over the smoke. In less than four seconds he sneezed.[7] His circulation was restored, and the healer charged me four pounds for his efforts.[8] I took it as a great lesson which I have never forgotten. When all was over, my master called me to his bungalow, and putting his hands on my shoulders, he said: 'Look here, headman, never punish when you are angry!' I knew that if I had been taken to the police, I would have been severely dealt with. The advice I wish to whisper into your ears is: 'Never punish when you are angry!' You are not dealing with grown-ups, but with children whose training in their respective homes differs. Some are properly trained in their homes, others are being spoilt at home, and that is the reason they have been sent to you for good and useful training. You must be vigilant and patient at all times else you can never succeed in being a good teacher."

The teacher again said: "Thank you, Sir. You have lit the

---

[7] This is the same story that Obeng tells of his own childhood in his short autobiography.

[8] Again Obeng seems to have forgottern what he has already narrated: namely that he saved all his money with his "Master", while at Obuasi.

candle of my mind."

"I am glad I have," said Akrofi. "The candle of your mind has been lit by the hand of my power; extinguish it not with the contrary winds of desires and passions. The healer of all your troubles is remembrance of me; forget it not. Make my love your capital, and cherish it as the spirit of your eyes!"

The schoolboys, not knowing what advice and chastisement had been given to the teacher, began to play truant, out of fright, but by the tact and patience of the headmaster, the discipline, the punctuality and regularity of the children were restored. The school continued to flourish, and its fame spread with lightning speed far and wide.

Akrofi's wealth, coupled with his kindness, attracted many people and many things to him and his village, in the same manner as white ants carry soil from many parts of the country to make their anthill.

When Akrofi was so securely established, he made up his mind to build himself a house at Abetifi. A plan of a very nice type of European house was made for him. He arranged with some sawyers for wood, and after sufficient had been stored, he debated in his mind as to what material — stone or cement — was to be used for the actual structure. He decided in favour of cement. Cement blocks were produced, and brick-layers were ordered from Kumasi for the work. These came with some good Fanti carpenters who made the doors, and windows. As everything was ready before the work was started, the erection was so rapid that every person who passed there stood and said how true it is that money on the other side of the Atlantic is called "the almighty dollar." All the workmen did their work so diligently that in a very short time the building was completed.

The large hall was thus painted: the ceiling with copal vanish; the top-wall above the top moulding was primrose and the middle wall painted with a green ochre mixture and the bottom wall with terra-cotta. A beautiful Axminster carpet covered the floor. The ceiling of the portico was painted with copal varnish, the top wall green ochre mixed with lime; the middle wall with cream paint and the bottom wall with red paint. The ceiling of the verandah was white, the walls yellow ochre, and lavender. The doors and windows were all painted French grey. The building was so nice that people from nearly all the surrounding towns visited it[9] and highly congratulated Akrofi on his exceptional good fortune.

At the top of the roof, Akrofi made two replicas of a cutlass in massive gold and wrote with silver letters the word EIGHTEENPENCE, which he fixed at each end of the roof showing the public that a cutlass that cost him eighteenpence was the beginning of his good fortune.

It was obvious that the central power of Akrofi's personal magnetism, which held together all what he possessed was nothing but industry which brought fortune in its train. This was the central power of the Attraction of Cohesion!

---

[9] Obeng is here describing his own house which he built in Abetifi with his mother's money. He called it *Kuru Memorial Villa*, in his mother's memory. The building is still in use today, but much neglected.

CHAPTER 18

The Ingratitude. Poor-No-Friend

WE HAVE heard that Akrofi's wealth attracted many people to him who claimed to be his relatives. Some were near, others remote relatives; others again were no relatives at all. Among the distant relatives came a certain man whose name was Kofi Dawoanom.

This man was never able to make two ends meet, he therefore deserted his town and country, and roamed from place to place like a murmuring and winding river. At first he went to Atebubu where he planted yams which he sold at Kumasi. There he made a good fortune, but through constant bickering with the towns-men, there was a conspiracy against him. He overheard this one evening when he was in the public latrine.[1] The conspirators planned that they would either frame a false charge against him which would drag him to court, where he would be fined heavily or imprisoned for more than six years, or put something in his store and charge him with stealing. The next morning, before cockcrow, he had decamped from the place.

He came to settle in Kumasi. Here he learned how to make beads. He modelled nice beads which had a quick sale. He had many customers who bought from him and retailed them as they were more popular than the European-made ones. He made much wealth from this industry. Seeing that he had amassed

---

[1] Text B has had this reference to a latrine removed.

enough capital, he made up his mind to open a small store and sell European goods. As there was too much competition in Kumasi, he moved to Tarkwa from where he used to go to Obuasi to buy from the Ashanti-Obuasi Trading Corporation. Here again, fortune smiled on his work, and afterwards he made up his mind to sell spirits. He applied and obtained a Government Licence which cost him ten pounds per annum, and which permitted him to sell spirits. He was there with his wife, whose name was Tipa.

One night after eight o'clock he went out to visit one of his friends whose name was Asare-Dua. He left his wife in the store. While he was away, there was a knock at the door, and thinking that her husband was returning, Tipa opened the door. It was not her husband, but a certain man, holding a small bottle. He asked her to be so kind as to sell a little rum to him to enable him to prepare some medicine for his son who was suffering from a very strong belly-ache. The woman replied that it was after nine o'clock, so she could not sell. The man, however, pleaded so hard and said that unless he got the rum in time, his son would die before dawn. This melted the woman's heart, and considering the condition of the patient, she gave the man what he needed to be able to prepare the medicine for the child, free of charge. The man pleaded with her to take his money, else her husband might suspect that there was an illicit friendship between them. She replied that she had no inclination to make any friendship, and her husband would never think such a thing; but because it was illegal to sell at that time, she refused to take the money; but there was no law prohibiting presentation.

The man sat and talked and smoked and the woman reminded him to go and attend to his sick child, for he had told her the illness was serious. On hearing this, the man bade her good night, and departed.

Not long afterwards her husband came in, and she told him that a certain man came to tell her that his son was suffering from a strong belly-ache, and intended to buy some rum to prepare some medicine for the patient; but as it was too late to sell, she had given him a little, free of charge. The man said nothing; but he afterwards asked the woman if she could identify the man by day. She told him that the man wore a hat covering half his face, so she could not; but she added that the man was a stammerer and a fast speaker, so she could make out the man by that. The more Dawoanom thought about the matter the less he liked it. He lay awake the whole night, and at cockcrow he told his wife that he had passed a very restless night, for two thoughts flashed through his mind about the gift of the rum which she made to the unknown man. To begin with, the man must be her lover, else she would not have admitted him into the store after nine o'clock. Secondly, if he was not her lover, she must have dealt with a policeman who had tempted her in order to get her to break the law. On hearing this, Tipa at once burst into tears. The man asked her why she cried, and she replied that either of these accusation, was a good reason for weeping. The first charge insulted her; whilst the second meant that they might be taken to court and fined for having sold rum at a wrong time. But the man's mind lay firmly on the first accusation; — illicit friendship.

Early the next morning, her husband went to consult his friend about the matter. That man told Dawoanom to watch in the morning to see if the man who was presented with the rum would come to thank her. If the man failed to do this, Dawoanom should expect trouble for then the man must have been a policeman in disguise. The friend's wife said that her husband's reasoning was lame; for it would be likely that the man would not come to thank the woman if they were friends, for he could not know whether the woman would report the matter to her husband or not.

While they sat pondering over the affair, a boy came to tell Dawoanom that a constable was looking for him. He got up and followed by his friend, he returned to the store. Here they found two policemen waiting. One of them asked Tipa to show them which man was her husband and owner of the store. She pointed out her husband, who was arrested and taken to the Criminal Investigation Office. There he was charged with having sold alcohol after hours. He was asked to apply for bail, on failure of which he would be kept in custody until he was tried. His friend signed a bail bond to the sum of ten pounds, and Dawoanom was allowed to go home after being told to come to court the following Monday.

When they reached home, Tipa was still crying. Her husband was now convinced of her innocence and begged her pardon for having entertained such a foul idea about her faithfulness. But she would not be comforted. She did not take her husband's apology; for it was much too painful to her that after eighteen years of marriage, the man should still doubt her conjugal fidelity. Besides she knew that, inasmuch as her husband was bailed for a sum of ten pounds, he would be fined not less than five pounds, which was a good deal of money to lose. These mingled feelings compelled her to weep; and she refused to take any food. Dawoanom asked some other friends to assist in soothing her; but she was obdurate, and, like Rachel, she refused comfort. The only things she asked for were water and kola, and she insisted on refusing any food until the case had been judged and her innocence proved in court.

Monday came, and at eight o'clock in the morning, Dawoanom and his friend appeared in court. The District Commissioner was there, and the Registrar called the case and read out the charge. Dawoanom pleaded not guilty. The policeman who had brought the charge went into the witness-box with one bottle of schnapps which had not been removed from its carton. He stated as follows:

"My name is Ali Bida. I am a police constable. Four days ago, I went for patrol in the street where dam man sell rum. I saw two men go there buy rum. I look, look, and saw plenty people go there buy rum. I count them and see twenty-ten men. All buy rum from dam store. The time be twelve o'clock in the night. I have no witness, so I say I go buy some myself. I was in mufti. I go there and see a woman in the store. The man

no day. I ask the woman to give me rum to buy. He bring
this one. He tell me say ebe ten shillings so I pay am ten shillings
and take am for house. I report the case to Softener[1] who tell
me say make me bring him for court. This all I know."

The District Commissioner looked at the accused and said:
"Any questions?"

Dawoanom said, "Yes, Sir. Ask the Police at what time he
went to the store."

"I say ebe twelve o'clock."

"Had he any timepiece with him or did he guess it was
twelve o'clock?"

"I had a timepiece in my pocket."

"You just told the Court that you were in mufti, why do
you say now that your timepiece was in your pocket?"

"I say I was not in mufti, for I was on patrol, I say."

"You say you bought this schnapps from my store?"

"Yes."

"I sell only rum in barrel and gin. I have not a single bottle
of schnapps in my store."

"You lie, plenty dey for your store. Your wife took this one
from a case and plenty dey there just now. I gave him one
ten shilling note and he change me nine shillings in silver."

Dawoanom was then asked to give his statement. He was
sworn and he stated as follows:

"My name is Dawoanom. I am a spirit seller. I own the
store which the policeman speaks about. Yesterday, after I had
closed the store at eight o'clock, I went to visit a friend of mine.
I returned about ten past nine, and my wife then told me that
a certain man had come to her to say that his son was suffering
from a strong belly-ache, and he wanted some rum to prepare
medicine for him. As it was late, she did not sell the rum to
him, but she presented some to him. The man pressed that she

---

[1] "Softener" is possibly an attempt at rendering 'Superintendent' in
     Pidgin.

should take money, but she said because of the illness, he should have the rum free, for the time was too late for selling. He then bade her good night and departed."

This evidence was a contradiction to that of the policeman. Besides, the policeman said he gave her a ten-shilling note and the woman gave him change of nine shillings in silver, meaning that the bottle of schapps he produced at court cost him but one shilling. The District Commissioner ordered that Dawoanom's wife should come to give evidence.

When she appeared, she was asked with what coin the man paid for the rum or schnapps. She said the man showed her a florin but she did not take it. He meant to buy one shilling worth of rum, but she gave him enough to prepare the medicine for the child. The District Commissioner called the policeman and asked him how much worth of rum he went to buy. He said two shillings worth and he gave the woman a pound note and she gave him change of eighteen shillings.

The District Commissioner asked a Sergeant to take the policeman to the S. M. O.[2] for medical examination. The following was the letter addressed to the S. M. O. It was a memorandum.

"Please examine Constable Ali Bida and inform me whether he is mentally unbalanced or not. He is giving some evidence at this court, but he keeps contradicting himself, and I am not in a position to know what to do with his testimony."

The S. M. O. took the Sergeant and Ali Bida to his consulting-room and interviewed Ali.

"Tell me your name."

"Bida."

"Only Bida?"

"No, I be Bida Kanjarka."

"What is your business?"

"I be Police Commissioner."

---

[2] Senior Medical Officer

"Are you a Commissioner of Police?"

"No, I drive my master."

"Who is your master?"

"The Softener."

"Are you a lorry or car driver to the Superintendent of Police?"

"No, you don't hear well. I say I be train-driver."

The S. M. O. therefore wrote to the District Commissioner as follows: "Have interviewed Ali Bida and found him medically unfit."

The demented constable, escorted by the Sergeant came back to the District Commissioner's Office, and the letter was handed to him. After reading it, he told the Registrar that the court should resume its session at once.

At half past two the court assembled again, and after addressing the court, the District Commissioner said the case had been dismissed, as the man who brought the charge was not sound in mind.

Dawoanom, his wife and his friends went home relieved and happy. But Tipa was still weeping, for though her husband had not suffered financially, except through his store being closed for a few hours, yet she was still upset because her husband had suspected her. A little time later, she became more cheerful and ate some food; but she asked permission to go home to see her relatives, for she had been away for several years. Not knowing what was in her mind, her husband said she could go for six weeks.

Tipa fully prepared herself and having taken leave of all her friends, she left one afternoon by the Sekondi-Kumasi train and passed the night at Kumasi. The next day she reached Nkawkaw where she boarded a lorry for Abetifi. When she arrived, her mother was surprised to see how lean she had grown. She explained that her husband had disgraced her, in that he had suspected an illicit friendship between herself and a certain demented policeman, and because of that she could not eat or sleep soundly, and because of this insomnia she had lost a lot of weight and been reduced to a skeleton. Both her parents were very sorry to hear such a nasty accusation against their daughter. Later, the father said it must have been only a transient impulse of passion on the part of their son-in-law; but not any deep-rooted jealousy that impelled him to doubt the conjugal fidelity of their daughter.

The next day, a telegram was sent to Dawoanom reporting Tipa's safe arrival, and asking him to come home at once.

He left Tarkwa almost immediately the message was read to him, for he could not comprehend the purpose of so sharp a command. Via Kumasi he arrived home the day after his departure, and met his wife safe and sound. Towards evening, his parents-in-law took him to his father before whom they told Dawoanom the reason why he had been summoned to come home. He calmly admitted the charge, and patiently explained that he had not the slightest doubt of his wife's faithfuness; the thought had flashed through his mind and in an unguarded moment he had allowed his hasty tongue to say it. When he found that he had done wrong, he had begged to be forgiven before giving her permission to come home.

But the parents and Tipa would not agree to any amicable settlement, and that same night the marriage was dissolved. Dawoanom allowed Tipa to keep all the presents he had made her during the period of their marriage, and gave her a portion of a cocoa farm which yielded eighty loads of sixty pounds weight, as well as raw cash amounting to fifty pounds.[3]

Dawoanom returned the next morning to Kumasi quite boozed, and to Tarkwa the next day. He found that during his absence thieves had broken a window into his room and carried away everything that belonged to him. He could not carry on there any more, so he removed to Sekondi. After a stay of two months, he moved again, this time to Cape Coast; and a fortnight

---

[3]   Text B says five pounds.

later he went to stay at Elmina. After six months' stay, he fought
with a member the Stool family there; some sheep were slaughtered, and he was fined nine pounds and six shillings, or in
default: three months' imprisonment with hard labour. He could
evidently not pay the fine, so he went in for the three months
and when released, he went to Anomabo.

One bright moonlit night he was conversing with some men
under a shade tree, and told the people that he had heard that
some time back, King Osei Asibe Bonsu of Ashanti attacked the
town and defeated the King of Anomabo and killed him and
carried off his head to Ashanti. The victorious king went so far
as to attack a steamer which was on the roads, and wished to
shatter it to pieces, hence his surname Bonsu, meaning 'The
Whale.' The last word scarcely left his mouth when he was
arrested and taken to the Palace where the case was settled against
him, and he was fined forty pounds and four sheep,[4] in default:
six months' imprisonment. He met a Kwahu traveller there who
paid the amount for him and obtained a promissory note from
him. In consequence of this unsettled and nomadic life, he could
not work for any money. He therefore became poorer and
poorer, and drifted to Accra, where he stayed for two weeks and
thence to Nsawam and again to Suhum and then hid himself
in a small village named Kayera, because of his numerous debts.
He had to find some means of evading his debts and to defraud
the public, so he changed his name and assumed the name of
Doku, and under this assumed name he travelled from place to
place. Even now, like the owl, he could not go out during the
day. He hid himself in the bush, and under a bedstead when
he was at home.

Akrofi and the other relatives heard of his misery, and sent
messengers to go and bring him home. They went with Poor-
no-Friend. Dawoanom had been with Akrofi when he bought

---

4 Text B says ten pounds.

the puppy. They had all played with it and stayed together for a long time,[5] so the dog knew his scent as well as it knew Akrofi's.

The people in the neighbourhood knew nobody who bore the name of Dawoanom. The messengers kept on going from one village to another, asking all the time if they knew a certain middle-aged man who answered to the name Dawoanom, but nobody knew or had heard of him.

One day they passed the night at one small and dirty village. At night they attended the public latrine.[6] There in the darkness Dawoanom had come to ease himself, and there he was scented by Poor-No-Friend. On recognising him, the dog howled and crouched at his feet. They followed the man, who was known as Doku, to his house. They asked him his name, and he confessed that his name was Dawoanom, but because of his many debts, he had changed his name to Doku. They asked him if he knew Akrofi, and he said he was Akrofi's uncle. They then told him that Akrofi had sent them to bring him home. They had brought sufficient money to cover all his debts. This having been done, he took his leave from all the people in the neighbourhood, and came home with the messengers. To his profound joy, he met Akrofi in the midst of plenty.

When Dawoanom came home, he had not a cent of his own. He was very kindly received and treated by Akrofi and his wife, and all the servants highly respected him because of his relationship with their master. His food and drink, of course, he received from Akrofi's table and he was additionally given pocket-money of five shillings a day. Besides, fine cloths, sandals, hats, singlets and all everyday necessaries were lavished on him; but Dawoanom expected more. Like the grave or the fire, he was never satisfied. He began to speak ill of Akrofi and his wife. His daily allowance was increased to ten shillings and then to

---

[5] One can only guess at the age of this dog by now.

[6] This reference to a latrine had been removed from Text B.

one pound, and he was told to report, if he found that the latter amount was insufficient. But Dawoanom would not report; saying that he was not a beggar to ask for anything before it was given to him. He openly spoke against Akrofi and said he had not an inch of respect for him and all his riches. He began to abuse the workmen, and ill-treat them. Next he quarrelled with the headmaster of the school, and told him he was not the only man who could teach, so he should go to his own country; and that by writing to Cape Coast, or to Accra, they could secure a better and a more competent teacher than a Togolander. The word 'Togolander' annoyed the headmaster not a little, and at once he submitted his resignation. With him went all his staff saying that if their principal were thus insulted, much worse would be in store for them. So there was a wholesale resignation of the teachers, and the school collapsed and was closed. All the good work done by hard toil of many years was destroyed by Dawoanom in one day. Nor was this all. Some of the labourers were badly treated. Some were beaten, others were rebuked and others insulted. One by one they resigned, so that in the course of six months half the town was deserted, and in another three months only a few people remained. The farm was about to revert to bush.

Then this disreputable and brawling man turned to Akrofi's wife and said:

"In this country every woman who marries goes back to her relatives. Because you have become a queen, you have never gone back to see your poor relatives, and you never have the mind to. Now that I am here, you will be destooled as queen. You cannot even go to the kitchen to cook for your husband; nor are you able to wash your husband's clothes. Be ashamed of yourself, you disgraceful and useless woman. If your husband were an inch wiser, he would not have married a rotten and useless woman like you. You have servants who are paid to do your house-work for you. Does your mother treat your father so? Or you think we are all fools? If the horse is a fool, the rider is no fool. If your husband is an idiot, I am not; and I will see that everything is in order in this town and especially in this house. Woe to the house in which the hen crows, and the cock is dumb! This will, no, this has come to an end just from this minute. You dare say one word to me, and your parents will see your brains dashed out!"

He was still speaking, when Akrofi called him aside and said:

"My dear uncle, I am very much sorry that you have behaved so disorderly to my dear wife, who is my all in all, my treasure, my everything on this earth. You have disgraced us before our own servants and the whole public. This woman married me when I had nothing which I called my own. She has been my helpmate, and my lucky star. She has helped me by her industry and good counsel. Without her you would not have met me in this condition. I therefore beg you earnestly, not to treat her so contemptuously."

Akrofi had not finished speaking before his uncle in a fit of fury interrupted him. He threatened Akrofi's life and said if he had allowed his wife to ride over him, and to enslave him, he, Dawoanom, could not tolerate such behaviour. If he had an atom of sense in his head, he would not have behaved in like manner.

The next morning Akrofi's wife asked his permission to visit her relatives. Akrofi could not part with his wife, not for one hour; but out of some mental pain, the woman insisted upon leaving, so Akrofi permitted her to go, though not without pain.

After her departure, Dawoanom seized Akrofi by the throat and flung him on a stone on which the labourers whetted their cutlasses. He fell with such a force that it gave him a serious head-wound. Some of the young boys in the yard used the remainder of the potassium permanganate with which the school boy had been healed, and when Akrofi was better, he made up his mind to leave the place.

CHAPTER 19

The Migration

AKROFI DECIDED to flee from his uncle, for the latter's temper and tongue were unbridled and uncontrollable. What pained him more was the absence of his wife, for without her, he became dejected and everything was dismal to him. But because of the family relationship between Dawoanam and himself, among the Akans, he feared he might be regarded as a bad man by those who did not know of the behaviour of the uncle.

When his wife arrived home so unexpectedly, her parents felt very uneasy, and her mother told her that she thought her visit was a foreboding of some change; for she brought no letter or greeting from her husband. Her younger sisters and their children who had not seen her before were struck with a fever of enthusiasm, but the father prophesied a dark and relentless future. The newcomer herself did not speak. It was then visible that she had reaped a harvest of barren regrets. Like the princess in the Arabian Nights, who was bewitched to become dumb for one year and one month and one day, this woman sat resolute and quiet, and nothing moved her to speak or sigh; not even her mother's entreaties and acclamations. The parents' astonishment grew greater and greater, and so they sent a courier with a letter to ask Akrofi in what condition his wife left him, on what terms he had parted from his wife and why she came unattended. In the neighbourhood it was whispered that she was losing her reason; others said she had stolen her husband's money and she had been sacked. Others again said perhaps her husband had married another wife and so jealousy had driven her home.

The courier did not go far before he met with a hired

messenger from Akrofi holding a letter addressed to his wife.
It read:

"My gentle dove; my rose without a thorn; my all in all;
my everything! My heart is rent in twain, for you know that
if a worm is cut in two, each end wriggles here and there, and
then lies motionless in death.[1] You are not unaware that you
and I have been rivetted together by love. You are not 'my better
half', and I am not yours; but we are our united better whole.
Without you I am not a half but a zero, and so I feel you are.
Return to me in two days to meet me alive or in three days to
see my grave. If you come at the time specified, I will drive
the callous and conscienceless brute from the house, so that we
may live as happily as before. All our lost fortune will return,
if not the double. If loneliness and love will not urge you to
come back, let not my letter."

The letter was read over and over, again and again, and the
sentence about 'the callous and conscienceless brute' clarified the
situation and told them that something untoward had been done
in the house by Akrofi's vagabond uncle who had arrived recently, and that had undoubtedly compelled their daughter to
leave her husband. The tone of the letter, too, demanded an
immediate reply, and a speedy return of the woman to her husband
in order to meet him alive. The woman could not be persuaded
to go back, but the last sentence of her husband's letter preyed
on her mind and heart. The messenger knew perfectly well that
if they did not go back in time, the consequences would not be
pleasant; but he did his best to hide this. The mother spoke
cheerfully to her and told her that the tone of the husband's letter
portrayed nothing wrong, therefore she would convey her back
herself. Then a faint, transient, wistful smile brightened the
wife's gloomy and brooding face.

Hasty preparations were made by the mother and her
servants; therefore Akrofi's father-in-law spoke privately to his

---

[1]   This rather grotesque simile has been omitted in Text B.

wife about the gravity of Akrofi's position. Both of them returned to the messenger and told him that they felt his attitude spelt despondency and melancholy though his exterior showed great calmness, and they begged him to tell them the real condition in which Akrofi was at the time of his departure.

The messenger then told them that in fact his master was quite nigh to death at the time of his departure; he had locked himself in his bed-room, packing and putting his things in order. He had accompanied him half way, and enjoined him not to disclose his condition to his wife, for he thought that that would give her much discomfiture. This accelerated their speed, and both father and mother accompanied their daughter to her husband.

They were conversing on the road as to what condition they would meet Akrofi in. The mother thought they had delayed too long after the arrival of the messenger, so she did not expect to meet him alive; but the father said so long as he had not heard from his wife, he would not budge, or take his life. Akrofi's wife was as silent as the fish; she sighed and sobbed intermittently as if her lips had been sewn together.

When they had walked half the way, the messenger sat down on the bank of a river to gulp down some of the food he had in his bag and drink from the river. When they were resting in the shade, they heard something like the snore of a man who had a deep and undisturbed sleep. The father hushed them, and when the noise was heard again, Akrofi's wife screamed and shrieked saying: "Help, father! My husband is dying!"

Off they darted to the spot whence the noise came. There to their horror, they saw Akrofi dangling at the end of a rope; his tongue protruding like that of a highly thirsty dog. With the speed of a squirrel, the messenger climbed up the tree and cut the rope. Luckily, Akrofi was not dead. It was just at the time they halted that he slipped the noose round his neck, but his neck was badly bruised and he could not utter a word.

They left all their personal effects, and with a native woven cloth, an improvised hammock was made, and Akrofi was carried by the messenger and his father-in-law. They did not go far before they were overtaken by some men, who being financially embarrassed had intended to go to Akrofi to ask him for a loan. They were six in number. They relieved the first carriers and slowly and quietly they moved forward.

You can imagine the condition of Akrofi's wife. She tore her hair and flung herself down and tumbled over and rolled forward and backward. She cried and yelled and was about to cut her throat with a knife she had been using in peeling an orange for her mother, had her father not quickly snatched it from her hand. They carried Akrofi back to the village of a farmer nearby. A physician was called who was very successful with his herbs, and in less than four days Akrofi was able to eat and drink a little. The bruises on his neck soon healed and exactly one week afterwards, he was able to tell them all that had happened which had driven him to attempt suicide. This was what he told them:

"A few days back, out of a profound anxiety I allowed my dear wife to leave me for a few weeks. She was torn from my heart and I was racked with sorrow. I was confined to my bed the whole day and the next, and I could not take[1] anything. My eyes were saturated with my tears and when I could no more control myself, my voice gave vent to utterances which expressed how I missed the woman. My uncle heard me, and came with the intention to see and to ask me what was the matter. As my eyes were wet, I did not like to open the door until I had washed my face. He became exceedingly annoyed when at the first knocking the door was not opened. Off he flew in a rage, and laying hands on an axe he struck the door with it and shattered it to pieces. I ran with all speed into the next chamber, fearing that he would dash out my brains. He then stood quietly behind that door for a short time; for I did not hear his foot steps. Not long afterwards I heard him descending the

---

[1] Eat anything.

flight to the ground floor. He returned, and I did not know what he was about. He had fetched a tin of kerosene with which he bespattered, nay, saturated the door and to which he lit a match. In a jiffy the whole building was in flames. He had already gone down again, to watch the end of his victim.

"I had to act quickly or I would be roasted in the flames. Therefore I decided to flee for my life. I jumped through the window and fell headlong onto the lawn below, into the pit the school boys dug not very long ago for the practice of long jump. Fortunately, nature carried me in her arms, and no harm befell me. I made off at once through the Para-rubber plot. As the roof fell in, I presume he went and raked among the ashes trying to see any traces of my burnt body. To his utter disappointment, he went round the burnt building and found there the impression which my feet had made on the lawn. These he followed.

"While I was confined to my room, I had packed all my valuables, and buried them under the cover of darkness at a remote corner of the farm; leaving nothing, not a dime, to the callous and conscienceless man. When I was then in the Para plot, hiding behind an ant-hill, I heard him howling like a mad dog who has seen a ghost in the night; and I held my breath. Thinking that he might see me at my hiding place, I crept like a snake attempting to conceal myself under the half-decayed log of a huge tree. But, when I got there, two amber snakes were fighting, and when they saw me, the victor turned and glided towards me as if I had intention to trespass in his domain. Ghastly death stared me in the face! In desperation, I ran away, but stumbled and fell in a hole at a place where a tree had been blown down by a fierce gale. In that hole I saw something like the fragment of a jar, but I had no time or eyes to examine it. I ran on again, and in my haste I stepped on a sharp thorn, and as I had no knife to remove it, it has since festered and caused my foot to swell. Oh, the pain that I have had because of it!

"In the circumstances, I could no more effect my escape, and as my uncle, by some miraculous means found my trail, and was overtaking me, I decided to take my life by hanging myself, rather than to fall into the hands of my merciless, malicious, ungrateful, blood-thirsty, and afflicted uncle.

"As soon as I had decided this, I climbed into a tree and hanged myself. At the instant I dropped down, my uncle came to the place, and seeing me struggling and dangling here and there, he attemped to hold my legs and pull me down to break my neck bone, and finish me, but owing to his stunted stature, he failed to reach me. He then exclaimed: 'It serves you right; I am relieved, and have from this hour become the only owner of everything in the domain that formerly belonged to you, the slave of a woman!' — and at which he went away. Just at this time you happened to hear me and came just in time to snatch me away from the jaws of death. You are my guardian angels.

"Now that I am a little better I pray that you, my loving esteemed parents-in-law, leave me and my dear wife alone. When I am fully recovered, we shall migrate to some place until we hear that my murderous uncle is no more. Before you go back, go to Para-plot, and from thirty-seven paces southwards from the ant hill, you will see a stone on which I have marked an X. Under that stone lies all our wealth which I buried before the house was burnt down. At some other place I buried sufficient money which my wife and I will use in our sojourn until, God willing, we come home again. But before we depart, please bring our young daughters to see us and to receive our blessing and perhaps our last advice before we leave."

A courier was sent for the three girls whose names were Violet, Lily and Rose, for I forgot to tell that Akrofi was baptised at Obuasi.[2] Akrofi sat and holding Violet, the eldest daughter by the hand, he said:

---

[2] Since Akrofi has made repeated references to the bible in the novel, one could have assumed that he was a christian. The essence of stressing this point now is that it would explain why his daughters carry European names. In Ghana, a 'christian' name is a non-Ghanaian name. Neither Lily, Violet nor Rose are biblical names.

"Let the modest violet be to you, my dear daughter, the image of humility and of the benevolence that does good in secret. It clothes itself in the tender colours of modesty; it prefers to bloom in retired glades; it fills the air with its fragrance while it remains hiding beneath the leaves. May you also, my dear Violet, be like the retiring violet, avoiding vain display, not seeking to attract the public eye, but preferring to even do good in quietude and peace. I commit you into the hand of the never changeable God, who will never leave you fatherless. *Au revoir!*"

The eyes of both father and daughter and all who were present were wet. Violet was released from the hold of the father, and she stood aside to give way to Lily. Akrofi held Lily by the hand and said:

"Let the lily, my dear daughter, be to you the emblem of purity. Look how beautiful, how pure and fair the lily is. The whitest linen is as nothing compared with the purity of its petals; they are like the snow. Happy is the maiden whose heart is as pure and free from stain. But the purest of all colours is also the hardest to preserve pure. Easily is the petal of the lily soiled; touch it but careless or roughly and a stain is left behind. In the same way a word or thought may stain the purity of innocence. Be obedient and respectful and be careful that you never soil your purity of character by anything untoward your name. Never do or say anything that you would not like to be seen or heard. I commit you into the hands of the never changeable God who will never leave you fatherless. *Au revoir!*"

Then turning to Rose, the youngest daughter he said:

"Let the rose, my dear daughter, be to you an emblem of innocence. More beautiful than the colour of the rose is the blush that rises to the cheek of a modest girl. It is a sign that she is still pure of heart and innocent in thought. Happy is the maiden, whom the suggestion of a thought that is indelicate, will cause to blush, as she is thus put on her guard against the approach of danger. The cheeks that blush readily will retain for a long time their rosette hue, while those which fail to blush at the least indelicacy of thought will soon become pale and wan, and go to the grave before their time. I commit you into the hands of the unchanging God who will never leave you fatherless. *Au revoir!*"

Akrofi then asked for some violets, lilies, and roses and tied them together in three posies and gave one to each girl, saying:

"The violet, the lily and rose, sister flowers as they are, belong one to another; they are incomparable in their beauty, and are rendered still more lovely by being together. In the same way, my dear daughters, are humility, purity and innocence close-linked sisters of virtue and cannot be separated. God designed that humility and purity should be the constant and faithful sisters of innocence in order that it may be the more easily preserved from danger. Remain humble, pure and modest, my dear daughters, and you will also remain innocent. Remember that unity is strength, that united, you will stand, but divided, you will fall. Bind yourselves, therefore, tightly together by the strong and unsoiled string of love and unselfishness. If you let the string soil or sag by avarice, envy and malice, and it breaks, be sure, your enemies will pounce upon you, tear you to pieces and devour you. May your hearts be ever pure like the snow-white lily and your cheeks will ever resemble the rose in beauty. Live pure, speak true, right wrong and follow your God and your King! My eyes are getting dimmer with tears and so I cannot speak any longer. Remember always what I have just told you. *Adieu!*"

After these words, Akrofi asked his parents-in-law to take his three daughters with them, adding that they might go to the spot he showed them marked X, and take anything that they needed. He also requested that the daughters should be trained like christian children though their grand-parents were heathen.

Before Akrofi's father-in-law departed, he poured wine into a glass with which he poured a libation and said:

"O Sky-God, whose day is Saturday, you who never fail those who trust in you, come and receive this wine and drink it. You Earth, whose day is Thursday, come and receive this wine and drink it. You Rivers and Streams, and you Trees and Climbers and Undergrowths, do assemble here, I pray, to drink this wine which I offer you now. You the Spirits of our Ancestors, who look after us and guard us daily, protect us from all harm and evil, I beseech you, come and receive this wine and drink it.

"Akrofi has married my daughter, and they live happily together. They have given us three grandchildren[3], and we have hopes that they will have more. But because of the unbearable conduct and behaviour of Akrofi's uncle, they have been compelled to migrate from this country to an unknown country. I beseech you on their behalf, for good protection from all sorts of troubles or accidents or evil. Guard them from their enemies and from treacherous friends, guard them from ill luck and from sickness. Break their hard luck. Do not suffer a tree to fall on any of them or a snake to bite any of them. If they reach a village or town where they are inclined to halt or settle, let the people of the place love them and stay with them peacefully. If they farm or choose to do any other work, stand firmly behind them; and let success crown their efforts. If they get children, I pray on my knees, that the children be robust and healthy and obedient. If there be any persons whose mind is to entrap and bring them into any trouble, I pray, let the calamity or the trouble turn against ill-disposed persons. Those who will determine to seek their downfall or destruction when they have not done them any harm, let them be punished, I kneel and urgently pray that those ill-disposed persons die prematurely to nip their designs in the bud.

"Bless my son-in-law and my daughter abundantly and bless everything that they do, and send them home rich and prosperous. Do not let any of us become deaf or blind or impotent or

---

[3]   So Akrofi's other children, Sam and his brothers, are not the offspring of this marriage.

barren. Bless us all who have met here and preserve our lives. But those who hate us and seek our destruction, let us drink wine at their failing; let us dance on their graves!"

The wine was poured spasmodically as he spoke, emptying the glass with the last word, and the men who were there jointly chorused: "Well said!"

The old man and his wife and Akrofi's three daughters then departed and left Akrofi and his wife and their faithful servant, whom they called "John", because of his faithfulness. These communed together and decided to try to make a new home for themselves at Gye-yekita-wo-nsa[4] if they could stay there.

Faithful John carried their only portmanteau, containing their every day needs. The money they took, which was mostly in currency notes because of the weight, was in a hand-bag carried by Akrofi's wife.

After twenty days' walk at the rate of seventeen miles a day, they arrived at Gye-yekita-wo-nsa, where they lodged with a certain man whose name was Odiasempa. This man received and treated these exiles with all possible generosity. A small room, measuring ten by eight feet was given them which on the first night, they shared with John. The next day another small room, much smaller than what they occupied, was rented for John at the rate of one shillings per week. Akrofi told his land-lord that he had the intention to stay longer, should they find some work to do; therefore they wanted to hire two rooms. They were then shown a small apartment of two more spacious rooms in the same compound. The rooms measured twelve feet and fourteen feet by thirteen feet, and each was fitted with good windows and furniture. Here, thrilled with a sense of strange adventure, Akrofi and his wife remained peacefully and quietly for four long years. They asked their land-lord for a small piece of land on which they farmed and grew yams, garden-eggs, beans, and corn.

---

[4] Literally: 'unless we guide you', 'unless we hold your hand.'

They did this in rotation so they did not bring much more land under cultivation, to the surprise of the inhabitants who always had to find fresh land for their shifting cultivation.

Let us cast a retrospective glance to see how Dawoanom was faring in his new kingdom.

You remember when he was in a fit of frenzy, he set fire to Akrofi's house. When he met Akrofi suspended at the end of a rope between heaven and earth, he exclaimed that all his nephew's property was now his. But when he went back, the fire had spread mercilessly and devoured everything in the village. Now he had nowhere to shelter himself from the weather and from the wild animals. He went to a distant village to seek shelter from some sawyers until when he could erect a small house; but they had heard how ungratefully he had treated Akrofi and his wife and turned them out of their home, so they would have nothing to do with him.

He roamed here and there, exposed to all the rigours of the season. Hunger, cold and anxiety reduced him to a skeleton. No human being would give any favour or show any kindness to such a man. I need hardly say he repented his conduct, for the opportunity neglected commonly brings repentance; but it was too late. He could not undo the past; done was done, advice was too late. Dawoanom was old and deserted, and there was not a soul to whom he could turn for help. He had nobody to look after him or to appeal to or to do anything for him or to give him anything. Like Judas Iscariot, his conscience troubled him not a little, nay , it tormented him, and to find a quiet place from this painful sentiment, he committed suicide by hanging himself. Even there was nobody to pay him his last respects, and his mortal remains were eaten by hyenas. Such was the tragic end of the callous and conscienceless Dawoanom, an example of ingratitude.

In the meantime after four years' stay, one of Akrofi's headmen, who had wandered here and there, and had crossed mountains and dales in search of his master, happened to accidentally arrive at Gye-yekita-wo-nsa. At the outskirt of the town he saw a fine garden laid out in European lines, and which had been divided into various portions with lantana hedges which had been beautifully trimmed. In the garden, various crops had been grown in nice apple-pie order. The headman stood and gazed in great wonder and surprise.

Somebody asked him why he stood gazing at the garden with the look of a bushman[5]. He replied that the garden looked as if it were cultivated by his master, whom he was seeking. When he was asked what his master's name was, and he replied that 'Akrofi' was his name, the other man told the headman that the garden belonged to a certain stranger who had lived in the district some four years and who answered to the same name. The headman inquired where the stranger's house was, and his informant pointed out a bungalow on the side of a beautiful hill towering over the town which was called 'Jehova-Jireh' and was surrounded by fine gardens.

When Seidu, for that was the name of the headman, saw his master, he fell on his knees at his feet and cried.

"O master, for four long years I have walked here and there in search of you. I have good news to give you. Your uncle, that cruel man who drove you away from your country, died just a few months afterwards. Before he died he was reduced to a skeleton by poverty and hunger. Nobody cared for him and nobody gave him food or shelter. His cloths became torn or threadbare and as he had no friend or relative, he committed suicide. Nobody buried him and the dogs and hyenas devoured him. We all felt vindictive because of the inhuman treatment he gave you.

"After his death, I found some of your scattered workmen and gathered them, and we have now cleared the ruins of your town as well as the farms. Houses have been erected and the

---

[5] In Ghanaian parlance, 'bushman' refers to a person 'from the bush', who is uncouth, rustic, unpolished.

teachers who went away have returned. The school has been reopened there. Crops of cocoa, kola, pears, oranges and all what we have produced have been sold and all the money obtained from the crops is in safe-keeping, and the schoolmaster is keeping a regular account of all the transactions. The school now accomodates many more children then formerly. You will be pleased to hear that the School Inspector has visited the school three times, and the headmaster says his official reports of the school are very satisfactory. The Director of Education has sent money for the upkeep of the school, and this has been placed in the bank. The children have also been sent sports materials, which have made the school much more attractive than it used to be. Because of all these things, I have come to beg you to return."

Akrofi told Seidu that the news he brought was not wholly pleasant, because of the deplorable death of his uncle. He and his wife wept bitterly and mourned for Dawoanom for some days.

After a few weeks had passed, Akrofi presented his bungalow and farms to his kind landlord, and in addition gave him ten pounds in cash and promised to visit him again if opportunity allowed. Then, bidding good-bye to this friend and to everybody in his part of the town, Akrofi left for his old home.

His party arrived there safely and saw that all Seidu had told them was correct. What surprised Akrofi most of all was that the headmaster had engaged an expert building contractor, who had erected a new and most beautiful mansion. The key of the stately house was given to Akrofi, and he embarked upon a tour of inspection. Every room boasted of carpets and furniture. Electric lights shone here and there, and to the returned exiles it seemed like a fairyland. Their happiness and wealth was a hundred times greater than ever before. Akrofi greeted everyone in the village and thanked them heartily for what they had done for him while he was away; and when the money received for the crops had been given him, he bestowed gifts on them all.

Three weeks after their arrival, the couple went to visit their parents. But, alas, they were dead! Akrofi's sadness was trebled. A grand funeral was held in their honour. Fortunately, the three girls, Violet, Lily and Rose, were in the best of health, and returned happily to their old home.

Some months later, Akrofi remembered that when he was fleeing from his persecutor, like David before Saul, he had found in a hole what appeared to be a fragment of a jar. He took some of his men, including Faithful John and Seidu, and they went in search of it. When they discovered the spot, the jar was still there, and proved to be much larger than the first one. Seidu and the other men carried it home. It had been sealed up, so nothing was lost, In the house it was opened, and to the delight of the family, they found it was filled to the brim with pure refined gold.

Akrofi and his wife led a life of happiness, enjoying their wealth, and were kind and compassionate to all who were fortunate enough to fall in with them.